"We know you are watching us," the note read. "Are you one of us? We really hope that you are, and we would like to meet you. If you are interested, we will be at the address below after seven this evening. We would love to meet you." The address was written at the bottom. There were no names on the card, or a return address, but the stationery was heavy and very expensive.

It was too good to be true! She was usually shy about meeting new people, but she was just dying to introduce herself to these two women who had turned her on so much.

PROVINCETOWN SUMMER & OTHER STORIES

LINDSAY WELSH

First Magic Carpet Inc. edition February 2002

Published in 2002

Manufactured in th United States of America
Published by Magic Carpet Books

Magic Carpet Books
PO Box 473
New Milford, CT 06776

cover design: stella by design contact: stellabydesign@aol.com

TABLE OF CONTENTS

PROVINCETOWN SUMMER

The streets of Provincetown are old and the buildings hug up to them the way I curve into Leslie's body late at night. The salt of the ocean water is the taste of her skin in the lazy, hot afternoons, with the fan revolving overhead and a glass of ice and lemon by the overstuffed sofa. The grass that grows up through the sand sways as gracefully as she does when she collects shells on the beach at low tide.

I sit on the sand and watch her with a hollow feeling in my chest. Her lovely small breasts move slightly under her thin shirt as she reaches down to pick up a shell. She comes down almost every day to collect shells at low tide, then returns to her studio where

9

she turns them into exquisite little souvenirs for the tourists who come to Cape Cod each summer. They are extremely popular, and I can see why; they are as sensuous, as windswept, as much a part of the ocean and the beach as Leslie is. I see her moods in the bright strokes of paint she adorns the fragile shells with. In the winter, she paints stunning canvases, but it is the seashell trinkets, along with an occasional spot as a waitress or grasscutter when funds get low, that pay the rent and keep the refrigerator full.

Provincetown, Massachusetts is her year-round home, which is proudly announced on the bumper sticker that is probably the only part of her car that isn't rusty, to differentiate her from the tourists and the summer people who live on the tip of the Cape only when the weather is good. I am one of these. I come here each year in the late spring, with boxes of books and my trusty typewriter, from the small trailer park in Florida that is my home base. I love Provincetown with a passion. I love its weather-beaten gray houses, its clamshell-lined driveways, and especially the fact that I can be openly lesbian and not have to hide. My downfall is the winter here, when fierce icy storms rage across the sand dunes and the temperature drops to the point where cars—and I—won't start.

I cannot tolerate the winters, which seem to rejuvenate Leslie after a summer of heat and humidity. She thrives on the cold, and basks in the tight community spirit that fills the residents left behind when the throngs of summer people pack up and leave. So each fall we say good-bye, like college lovers, and I make my way back down the coast to the palm trees and the warm December days, when I can go outside in slippers and T-shirt to pick up my morning paper. Leslie remains behind, sending letters, painting pictures. I do not know if she has lovers when I am gone; I do not ask, and she does not ask me. But each spring, when I return to the apartment over the art gallery, which I have rented for the last seven years, we are just as if the winter had never happened, as if nothing had ever torn us apart.

I look out over the sleek sand, a sight not much different than that of my other home far away. Here, though, there is more for me. Barefoot, bent over, her creamy ass tight against her shorts, Leslie makes me want to run over the hard-packed sand and take her right there, in the salty foam and seaweed. I am on a high today; the book I have been slugging away at for almost a year is only a few days from completion.

The nights are a little cooler now, though, and the streets are not as crammed with tourists as they were in July. Leslie and I are both fiercely stubborn; she will not come to Florida, for she loves the different seasons, and I cannot remain here. Instead, we choose to fill our summers with intense, frequent lovemaking, if only for a short time, and go our separate ways when the long winter is inevitable.

Most of our friends think we are totally hopeless, and in the fall when I hold her tight and my tears spill out onto her hair, I think they are right. I wonder why I can't give in and spend the winter on the ice-bound cape. But the separation becomes a breathing space for us, and in spring when I return, feeling a little foolishly like the swallows, it is as if I have never left, and we continue our summer love just as feverishly as before.

Her bag filled with shells and stones, Leslie comes back from the water's edge. We get on our bicycles and return to town. She lives on the upper floor of an old frame house a few blocks from the commercial center of the town. The smallest room is her bedroom, the next largest a combination of living room and dining nook, with a tiny kitchen off to the side. The largest room, with one wall almost completely filled with wooden-framed windows, is her studio, which is always filled with a mishmash of completed painting, works in progress, seashells, glue, paintbrushes and a photograph of me, in a silver frame, on one wall. I am moved by the prominence of my picture, but in my orderly fashion, I can never figure out how on earth she turns out anything from the mess of materials that are cluttered on the tables and floor.

Even though we are together at some time almost daily, both of us need solitude to work, and when I write or she paints we leave each other alone. Hence the need for separate apartments, although it isn't uncommon that one of them is empty throughout the night. Sleeping with her and feeling her smooth, warm body pressed against mine is one of the joys I have with her, especially when we incorporate some sex into our morning coffee routine.

We put the bicycles on the porch and I follow her upstairs, enjoying the sight of her beautiful ass above me as she walks. She leaves the bag of shells sitting on the table and puts her arms around me. We kiss slowly, and she reaches under my shirt to run her fingers around my nipple. I push my tongue into her mouth, wanting more.

I kiss her throat, the back of her neck, the sweet spot by her earlobe, her silky eyelids and brush the tip of my tongue against her temples. I love to hold her like this. Her skin is still warm from the sun and tastes slightly salty, as if all the ocean has swept over her. I reach into the back pocket of her shorts to cup her firm ass cheeks, knowing how lovely they look naked and pressed up against me. She reaches down to hold my ass and we stand for the longest time, fingers kneading firm flesh, kisses planted on anything we can reach.

Leslie moves away, smiles at me and slowly, seductively, removes her shirt. She wears no bra, and her small, firm breasts cry out for attention. I sit her down in the overstuffed chair, then kneel before her.

My tongue finds her nipples instinctively. I love to suck them in, one at a time, then run my tongue slowly around each one while it's still between my lips. I bite them gently, pulling on them, nibbling at them, still flicking my tongue over the tender tip I hold between my teeth. I run my hands up and down her slim body, over her breasts, and down to tease the spot between her legs that feels warm and salty even through her shorts. I move back up to her lips, and she takes my fingers into her mouth, sucking at them, pushing her tongue between them. It makes me weak with desire for her.

I lean back, and she reaches down to help me pull off her shorts and panties. Her pussy is a lovely, sweet oasis between blonde-haired lips, and I could stare at it all day. I trace the designs of the folds with the tip of my tongue; she sighs, and I know so well the sweet electric tinglings that must be rising from my touch.

I probe with my tongue and hands, and my finger reaches the sweet nub of flesh at the top. Leslie groans. Quickly I replace my finger with my tongue. As always, she tastes both raspberry-sweet and salty at the same time, and I lap at the moist folds eagerly. She holds my head and pushes me deeper into her. I stick my tongue as far into her hole as I can, fucking her with it. Her hands in my hair set up a rhythm and soon my tongue is sopping with her lovely juices. My face is wet and all I can smell is the perfume of her nectar. I would love to drown in her pussy if I could.

I enjoy teasing her. I move up and lash my tongue over her clit, until I can feel her tighten up, ready to come. Then I return to her hole, lapping with long strokes, and she relaxes, moaning. I go back to her clit, kissing it, sucking at it, and again when I feel her getting close I leave it, so that she collapses in the chair, nearly at the edge of orgasm. Finally, after several long minutes of teasing her cunt, I go back to her clit and center all of my attention on it, licking, flicking, lapping.

I know Leslie's responses as well as I know my own. All of her muscles tighten, and even her toes curl up. She pushes her pussy against my face, rubbing herself on the tip of my tongue. My tongue and her sweet clit are one. When she comes, she is very vocal, crying out, pushing me into her, shaking. My own cunt is throbbing as I lick every last quiver out of her. I know exactly how good it felt.

Although she is still gasping for breath, she is on me in a moment, opening my shirt to reach my sex-swollen breasts. She knows how much I love to have them touched, and she leads me into the bedroom so that I can lie down. She takes forever on my tits. She kneads them, kisses them, licks at them, rubs them together, pushes them so that they touch and then licks the cleft in between. She knows my cunt is begging to be touched, but she refuses. Instead, she snakes her tongue down there, licks the insides of my thighs, and stops just inches away from my clit. It is my reward for teasing her, and she won't even allow me to brush my pussy with my hand for relief. Instead, she goes back to sucking my nipples and pushing her tongue into my mouth.

My skin is alive and on fire with each touch of her brilliant fingers and tongue. Leslie is an expert at lovemaking, and it is a joy just to lie back and submit to her will. She paints fanciful designs on my belly with her tongue, coming closer to my hot mound with each sweep.

When she finally touches my clit, I cry out with pleasure. She has somehow managed to focus my whole body on this point, and she shows me no mercy as she licks and sucks me. Her tongue is hot and wet between my legs, licking my clit, her hot breath playing on my aching skin. She pushes her finger into my hole as she licks me and begins moving it in and out, fucking me with her hand. It drives me wild and I cry for her to lick me harder. Her hand moves faster, her fingers deep inside me, her whole hand wet with my juice, her tongue lapping at me. My orgasm catches me by surprise. The wave of feeling moves right out to my toes and fingertips. When it is finished, I cannot bear to have her touch me. It is as if my skin is gone, and the nerves are on the edge of my flesh. Like her, I quiver and shake, and finally calm down in the loving circle of her arms.

The problem with making love in the early afternoon, of course, is that not much else gets done the rest of the day. With the cool sea breezes coming in through the window and both of us basking in our orgasms, we fall asleep in each other's arms. When I finally wake up, the shadows from the plants in the window are stretched long across the floor.

I try to get up without waking her, but it is no use; her enormous blue eyes open as soon as I sit up. I hold her tightly and kiss her beautiful lips. Our bodies are cooler now and it feels good to press against her, our breasts held tightly together, our pubic hair mingling. She brushes a lock of dark hair out of my eyes and kisses me again.

We dress and walk downstairs; I have offered to

treat for dinner. We walk along the house-lined street, hand in hand, and every now and again I stop to admire the front yards. In Provincetown, gardening seems to be a way of life, and almost every house is decorated with beautifully kept, colorful flower gardens. Their vibrant shades contrast sharply with my Florida home, where houses are more commonly landscaped with palms and shrubs. The colors remind me of Leslie, so vibrant and alive. She often paints the rich gardens and it seems as if she puts her soul into the colors too; one of her gardens hangs in my trailer where it brightens my isolated winter months.

We stop for dinner in one of the many open-air sidewalk restaurants. Over an aperitif she tells me about an idea she has for a new painting, and I feel a quick pang when I realize it will probably be finished and sold before I return in the spring. Many of her paintings are sold out of the gallery below my apartment, and when she is busy working I sometimes wander downstairs and study them. Like her seashell trinkets, I can see her in them: sensuous, earthy, firmly attached to this piece of land that juts sharply out into the bay. Her works are so unlike my writing, with its wanderlust, its ever-changing horizons.

Feeling like a tourist, I order a clambake dinner. I am still high from our afternoon sex, yet I want her again so badly my pussy throbs and I rub against the hard plastic chair. Still, I am tempered by the knowledge that our summer is coming to a close, and I know how hard it will be to say good-bye to her. I take out some of my frustration by cracking the steamed clamshells sharply in half, and breaking the lobster shell loudly with the steel crackers.

Leslie enjoys a much quieter dinner of crab cakes. Each time she lifts the fork to her lips, her tongue darts out first to meet it. I can feel myself getting wet and swollen at the sight, and I imagine that tongue in my mouth, in my pussy, against my hard, aching nipples.

She sees the look in my eyes, and reaches under the table to squeeze my knee. The tablecloth is very long and with a mischievous grin, she lightly runs her fingernails up and down my thigh, putting her finger under the edge of my shorts to tickle the skin underneath.

Gradually she moves her hand up further. My lobster is quickly forgotten. Under the cover of the tablecloth, she twists her hand to push my legs apart, then moves back and forth near my crotch in her lovely, teasing manner. I can hardly believe I'm sitting in a crowded restaurant with Leslie's hand near my cunt, and I pick up my wine glass and sip at it in a foolish attempt to look natural.

The waiter comes by and asks if everything is fine. Still with her impish grin, Leslie answers yes and at the same time, rubs her thumb over my swollen clit. The waiter glances up at my sharp intake of breath, but I smile and nod at him. I am relieved when he moves away to another table. Leslie winks at me, like a schoolgirl playing a prank, and takes a forkful of her dinner. Meanwhile, her other hand is busy teasing and stroking my throbbing pussy.

She starts rubbing my clit right through my shorts, which are very thin, and I can feel each flicker of her finger over me. I am having a hard time holding still. I want to writhe on her hand, squirm in the seat, push her hand against myself and hold it tight to me. Leslie knows this, and she is having a grand time watching me trying vainly to control my movements. I warn her that she will be teased without mercy for this. She only laughs and increases the motion on my hot button.

I can feel the heat from my belly right down to my

thighs. Leslie plays me like an instrument, knowing just when to rub hard and when to pull back and gently caress. Any attempt at sipping my wine is forgotten. I feel as if the whole restaurant must know what's going on, but I'm beyond caring. All that matters is my lover's hand touching me. I tighten up, so close, so close, and then the hot, sweet wave rises up out of my pussy and moves up my spine in a rapid, blissful sweep. I bite my tongue to keep from crying out as I come. Leslie's hand rubs every last wave out of my cunt, and I can feel that my shorts are soaked with my hot juice.

I struggle to pull myself together. Playing the saint, but with a canary-swallowing grin, Leslie is now eating her carrots, the picture of poise and manners. Orgasms always relax me and I seem to need all of my strength just to lift my hands and finish eating my dinner. Luckily for me the lobster is done, for the effort would have been far too much to handle. The potato is work enough at this stage.

When coffee comes, Leslie orders a slice of cheesecake, and is right back at it again, nibbling at it and running her tongue over the fork when she slides it out of her mouth. She is an angel to me; no woman I have ever met loves sex as much as she does, or makes me want her more. When we are together, I feel as if our only purpose on earth is to love and satisfy each other.

It is dusk by the time we finally finish. The streetlights are on and the shop windows are lit up, all of them open until very late to catch the tourist trade. The streets are alive with people walking along the sidewalks and up the middle of the narrow, one-way street. We decide it is too nice a night to let slip away, and we go for a stroll ourselves.

Provincetown was built for walking. Cars defer to

pedestrians here, and drivers will usually follow a group of walkers slowly down the road rather than honk and demand that they move. Bicycles are of course another matter, and Leslie and I check carefully for any before we cross over the street. The sidewalks are wide and couples walk arm in arm, men with men, women with women, women with men. There is an easy summer feel to the place, mixed with an almost overwhelming sexual satisfaction. On a warm night like this, it feels as if everyone in town is going to be happily fucked before dawn, no matter what their preference.

We stop off in the bookstore, where both of us buy a couple of volumes. We chat for a while with the shopkeeper, who knows us well—both of us seem to spend half our income on books. When we leave, we run into another pair of friends who invite us to a nearby bar for a drink.

The bar is cool and dark, with jazz playing quietly on the sound system. I am torn in my desire; I enjoy sitting and talking with our friends, but I am dying to get home and pay Leslie back for making me come in the restaurant. As we are sitting down, I brush against her and take advantage of the opportunity to tweak her nipple. She gives me a sultry smile across the table and I know she is just as eager to be paid back.

We order a carafe of wine. Our friends are a bit older than we are, two women who have lived together in Provincetown for years. Leslie sees them frequently over the winter, and often has dinner with them. As for me, they are two of the people I am sorry to leave when I make my trip back south.

As we talk, I can't keep my eyes off Leslie. A year younger than me, her blonde hair is bleached almost white from the hours of scouring the beaches for shells. She has the lovely outdoorsy look of people who live with hot summers, icy winters and the relentless tides. Her breasts are small and firm; I can still feel her nipple hot under my fingers. Her legs are long, her feet thrust into well-worn sandals. She still wears her thin shorts, and my eyes trace up the lines of her bare thighs to where they meet at her honey-rich, blonde pussy. I can picture how beautiful it looks, and I long to be there, rubbing my fingers, licking with my tongue....

I feel a hand on my arm, and realize that I have been spoken to but am off in my sexual dream world. All three of them laugh. I explain that I'm tired because of long nights pummeling my book into shape, but Leslie smiles knowingly at me. It's not much of a secret, what I'm actually thinking about.

It seems to take forever for the wine to be finished. I engage in conversation, but all the time, my mind is riveted on making love to my Leslie. Two women at a nearby table lean over it so close that their faces touch and they kiss gently; below the table they have their hands on each other's legs. I want desperately to touch Leslie like that. I can taste her juices in my mouthful of wine. In the midst of conversation she reaches over to take my hand, to make a point. Her warm skin is electric on mine.

Finally the wine is finished, and we beg off, explaining that I need some sleep. We kiss them good-bye and head back down the busy street to my apartment. On the way I lean over for a quick kiss, which turns passionate very quickly. Leslie is just as much in need as I am. We duck into a narrow alley-way between two stores. Her tongue is in my mouth immediately, probing and pressing against mine as hard as she can. She takes my hand and guides it between her legs. I can feel her wetness through her shorts, and her flesh seems on fire. She moans and rubs against my hand, her fingers on my breasts through my shirt. We grope like two sex-starved teenagers, kissing, feeling, grabbing each other with only one thing in mind. Reluctantly, I break away and take her hand, pulling her quickly along the crowded sidewalks. I can't get home fast enough, and Leslie keeps up with me.

There is a pleasant surprise waiting. The art gallery has rearranged its window, and one of Leslie's paintings hangs in front. It is a vibrant nude woman, her full breasts tipped with pink erect nipples, her hand gently exploring the dark triangle between her legs. The face is very abstract, but Leslie told me that she painted it while thinking of me. Seeing it out in the open, studied carefully by the people in the street who stop to look at it, makes me even hotter. I want to proudly tell them that it is my Leslie's work, that it is our wonderful sex set down in oils for everyone to admire.

I unlock the door and we go up the stairs, stopping halfway up for another long, passionate kiss. Usually I stop at my desk each time I enter the apartment, if only for a few moments, to proofread a page or add a couple of lines to the sheet that's always in the typewriter. This time, I ignore all of it.

We undress each other. Leslie comes up behind me and hugs me tightly. Her hands reach for me. Her right hand cups my breast. Her left hand moves down and her finger fits perfectly into the groove of my pussy lips. She plants delicate kisses on my neck while she fingers me. I reach behind and grab her ass cheeks, pulling her sweet mound close to my body. I can feel her heat from here.

She leads me to the bed. I make her lie face down on the comforter and kneel beside her. She loves to have her back rubbed as a prelude to sex. I start at her neck, rubbing gently, feeling her sweet skin move beneath my fingers. Gradually I work my way down her spine, kneading the soft flesh around her shoulders. Every now and again I bend down and trace the curve of her spine with my tongue, burying deep in the indentation just above her ass. She sighs and begs me to touch her pussy, but I tease her instead by just brushing the blonde hairs around it.

When I reach her ass, I spend a long time kneading her firm, creamy cheeks. Then I lean down and gently tongue the cleavage between them. She moans and lifts her hips to meet me. I brush her soft pussy hair again, this time with my tongue. As a final tease, I lick just once over her hot, wet cunt. She groans and rolls over, begging me to make her come.

It's too soon for that. Her beautiful tits are now facing me, and I waste no time in getting to them. I lick and suck at them, then push my own against them. Rubbing my nipples against hers gets both of us even hotter, and my pussy is throbbing with a will of its own.

She moans and kneads my breasts, and we deep-kiss for a long time, holding each other's nipples and rolling them between our fingers. Her touch sends hot shivers through me. I reach down and cup her steamy pussy in my hand.

Leslie pushes against my hand, trying to brush her clit against me. I touch the hot button quickly, brushing it with the tips of my fingers. She moans. She knows how to get to me, and plays with my nipples until I can't control myself any longer. I reach down and sink my tongue into her gorgeous cunt.

Immediately she bucks her hips up to push her clit against my tongue. Her pussy is as sweet as always. I take my time, using the very tip of my tongue to run under her soft folds all the way around to her lovely clit and hole.

She pulls at me, and I stop long enough to move over and straddle her lips with my own hot cunt. We both love "sixty-nine," and waste no time in feasting on each other. I like it because I am so busy concentrating on eating her, it takes a while for me to come and I can enjoy the achingly beautiful buildup even longer.

I am sure the gallery patrons below can hear us, we are moaning and lapping so loudly. For a while Leslie mirrors all of my actions. When I slow down and circle her pussy, she does the same to mine. Flicking my tongue hard across her clit brings the same hot flashes across my own. It is almost as if I am eating myself.

There is a new sensation now; Leslie's fingers are deep in my cunt, her tongue still on my clit. I love the full feeling, the way her thumb moves to brush against the folds of skin. I do the same to her. Her tight tunnel is soaked and feverishly hot. I fuck her with my fingers while I concentrate my tongue on her swollen clit.

Both of us madly enjoy our lickfest a little while longer. Then Leslie asks me to move down on the bed, which I do. Her hair dishevelled and her pussy wetly glistening, she positions herself opposite me, her legs crossed scissor-style over mine. Our two pussies touch and she begins to rub against me.

I push hard to match her frantic motions. I pull myself up on my pillow so I can see, and it's gorgeous. My own dark triangle grinds against her blonde one, clits nestled together, juices flowing. I love the scratchy feeling of her hair against me. She pushes hard and I gasp.

We start a regular rhythm. Hips bucking, soft

pussies grinding into each other, we moan and gasp at the waves of pleasure that course through our bodies. Her leg is stretched along my body and I take her foot, planting kisses on it. I push my tongue between her toes and she moans, grinding even harder. I match her movements.

We are moving so fast and hard I expect our cunts to burst into flame. Mine is already on fire, heating me, tongues of flame moving up my spine as her sweet bush crushes me. Both of us are sitting up now, taking in the beautiful sight of two cunts pressing together, dark and light hair, creamy asses, outstretched legs.

Leslie moves frantically and begins to cry out. She comes violently, her juices flooding my pussy. I have never felt so wet. She moans and shivers, enjoying every last wave, pushing against me. I get even hotter watching her come.

She waits for only a moment, then gracefully pulls away from me and kneels before my cunt, spreading my legs. Her practiced fingers begin to stroke my pussy. Her hand feels as good as her hot cunt did against my flesh.

She rubs faster and faster, her finger slipping over my soaked clit. Then she slips two fingers inside my hole, while her thumb expertly rubs the swollen button. She is a master, sliding in and out of my cunt, rubbing me, while her free hand reaches up to knead my breast.

I can't believe how intense my orgasm is. I seem to come from the very tips of my toes, and Leslie rides me out. Her thumb plays out all of it, until I am weak and gasping. Then she is in my arms, kissing my face, cupping my tender pussy with her hand.

I return her kiss. I can't believe how much I love her and how good she makes me feel. We lie together on the bed, our bodies covered in sweat and pussy juice. The smell of sex is heavy in the air.

Through the open window I can hear people talking as they walk by on the sidewalk. I wonder if anyone heard our loud lovemaking. I like to think that they did.

Gently, Leslie kisses me on the lips, then snuggles down within the curve of my arm, her head resting on my shoulder. One finger absently traces circles around my nipple. I turn my head and gently kiss her forehead.

There is no question of her staying the night; I am not about to let go of her right now. She pulls the light cover over us, since neither of us seems to have the strength to get up and close the window. We say a silent prayer to the inventor of the remote control, as I click on the small television that sits atop a bookshelf. We reject a talk show, a half-hour commercial for car wax and a police drama, and finally settle on my favorite movie, *Casablanca*, already halfway through. No matter, it's worth watching from any point. We both admit that we love Ingrid Bergman's clothes, sultry eyes and beautifully full, kissable lips, and not necessarily in that order.

Unfortunately, I miss my opportunity to see Bogie put her on the plane, for the next thing I know the early morning sunlight is streaming through the window and Leslie is clattering cups in my cramped kitchen. She kisses me good morning and deposits a cup of strong black coffee on the nightstand beside me.

Always an early riser, she is dressed with her cup of coffee half finished. She hugs me tightly and tells me she has to get home to finish a piece that the gallery is waiting for. My heart sinks when I hear the door close behind her, for the breeze coming through the open window has an end-of-season chilly touch to it.

I smooth the bed, pull on my jeans and take my coffee to the typewriter. Just after one o'clock, I am finished. Once again I am filled with the same conflicting emotions that I always feel when I start to pack a book for shipping to the publisher: elation that it's finally finished, but an emotional drain knowing that the work I've been doing for so long is over.

I call Leslie to tell her, but I get her answering machine. When she is working she turns it all the way down so that she can't hear the messages. I tell her there will be victory champagne later, then I wrap the book carefully for mailing and address it.

I walk into the downtown center with the precious parcel in my arms. The breeze is coming in over the ocean heavily, and it feels like rain, but I don't care. I mail the book inside the huge old post office building, then continue walking until I am out of town, up at the sand dunes that separate the waves from the road.

There is another couple walking along the beach, two women, arm in arm. I sit down on the soft sand and watch them. They stop to look at the sky and the waves, to pick up shells on the sand. They are an older couple, gray-haired but moving as gracefully as women half their age. They obviously know each other well, their motions complementing each other, their steps matching. I can see Leslie and myself together that way in twenty years, moving with the comfortable rhythm of people who understand each other perfectly.

Eventually the women gather their bicycles and walk back to the road, nodding a hello to me as they pass. I get up and walk down to the water's edge,

catching a glimpse of a shell half-buried. I pick it up
and rinse it in the ripple of water that moves up close
to me. I know Leslie would like it, and I slip it into
my pocket.

The air is very heavy and by the time I walk back
to the road, there is a thin drizzle falling. In the way
of seaside storms, it grows into heavy rain very quickly. There is no point in hurrying, and so I walk back
toward the town with the rain beating down on me,
my clothes soaked and sticking to my skin. When it
runs down my face it feels like tears.

The rain is still falling steadily when I get back to
my apartment. Leslie has obviously heard my mes-
sage on her machine, for she is inside the gallery,
looking through the open door and talking to the
owner. She tells me to hurry up and get inside to
some dry clothes.

It is difficult to peel the wet jeans off. When I do, I
remember the shell, and I give it to Leslie, who is fascinated with it. She has already started to run a hot
bath for me. I slip into the steaming tub, filled with
richly scented bubbles; the hot water on my cold
clammy skin is almost erotic.

When the bathwater starts to cool, Leslie comes
back in. She holds a large fluffy bathtowel and I let
her dry me off, almost purring with the luxury.
Finally she wraps me in my sinfully thick terrycloth
robe and we go into the kitchen.

She has brought steaks for dinner. Although the
kitchen is tiny we work well together, like trained
chefs. I boil rice while she washes vegetables and
arranges the steaks on the broiling pan.

When dinner is on the table, I open the champagne bottle with a flourish and pour two glasses. We
toast the book, then eat our dinners. Leslie tells me
about her painting, which is almost finished, and I

promise another bottle of champagne.

After dinner we clear the table and I run hot water into the sink. But before I can start washing dishes, I feel Leslie come up behind me and slip her arms around my waist. I turn, and meet her open-mouthed, sweet kiss.

The dishes are instantly forgotten as she unties my robe and opens it. Her hand slips down expertly to my breasts and fondles my nipples. I moan and kiss at her mouth, my hand slipping between her legs to feel her pussy through her jeans.

She breaks away and leads me into the bedroom. The familiar bed is inviting and we lie down together, kissing deeply and smoothing our hands over each other's creamy soft skin. I want to get inside her, in her mouth, in her pussy, under her skin, I love her and want her so much.

She is down and working my pussy over before I even realize it. The warmth from her wet tongue radiates through my thighs and up my spine. She licks me slowly, carefully, as if I am ice cream or a forbidden sweet treat. It is as hot and intense as the warm bathwater on my cold skin.

I can only groan and go limp with the pleasure. I let the delicious feeling of Leslie's tongue in my pussy take me over. She licks my thighs and the outer lips of my cunt, then zeros in on my clit with just the very tip of her tongue. Her touch is as light as her warm breath on me, and it tickles wonderfully, like she is stroking me with a feather.

She alternates for a while, rubbing my pussy with her fingers, then licking me slowly with her tongue. I love the motion of her hand, soft yet firm on my throbbing, wet clit, followed by the fluid movements of her swift tongue. I could lie back and take this for hours, it feels so good. She knows it, and she laps at me with long wet strokes from my hole right up to my clit. I shudder with each juicy sweep.

Leslie sits up for a moment and reaches for the glass of chilled champagne she has brought into the bedroom with her. She takes a mouthful and holds it for a moment, then swallows and returns to my aching pussy.

I gasp at the first touch of her icy tongue. Delicious little shivers course through me. I can hardly believe the sensation, her cold tongue and her hot breath mingling together on my cunt. Gradually her tongue warms up, and I cry for more. She takes another sip of the pale golden wine, and once again I am treated to her sweet cold tongue and warm breath, icy-hot between my legs.

My own mouth wants her now, to share this new feeling. Reluctantly she stops and stretches out in front of me. I take a sip from her glass, then move down to the blonde pussy that I want so very badly. Like me, she moans at the fiercely cold movement on her erect little button, and she asks for seconds when my tongue warms up again on her beautiful clit.

I sip more champagne, then bend down to her beautiful pussy. I can't get enough of her. I lick her pussy lips, nibble her clit gently. She moans and pushes against my tongue. I know from experience just what she likes best, and I give it to her, little butterfly kisses on her clit, my tongue stuck deep into her hole.

I want to make her come. I concentrate on her clit now, my tongue pressed against it. I can feel her excitement as she runs her fingers through my hair and pushes me deep into her sweet lips. Faster and faster I lick her, while she gasps and squirms on the bed. Finally she cries out with her release, her hips moving as I push my tongue into her.

Leslie begs me to kiss her, so that she can taste her

juices on my tongue. I move up on the bed and hold her close, kissing her and sharing what I have done with her. It is like sharing a beautiful intimate secret.

My own pussy is still throbbing sharply. As we kiss, Leslie's hand strays to it, and I moan at the first touch of her fingers. She plays with me, still kissing me. Our breasts are pressed tightly together and I love her hard nipples so close to mine.

She asks me to kneel over her. I do, positioning my pussy over her lips. She reaches up and grabs my ass cheeks, pulling me down to her mouth. The touch of her tongue on my swollen clit is magical.

She knows me as well as I know her. She licks the spots that excite me the most and then, when I am built up and almost overcome with the sensation, she concentrates on a less sensitive area. As always she loves to tease and on this afternoon she is doing a magnificent job.

Finally she flicks her tongue hard on my clit, the movement that she knows will make me come. It doesn't take long to build up the pressure that I feel just before orgasm. Leslie licks faster and the waves roll through my legs and belly, hot tingling flashes that are just heavenly.

I move down on the bed beside her, and we snuggle in together under the light blanket. It seems as if we have spent all of our time in bed the last few days. Leslie quickly agrees that it doesn't seem to be a bad way to pass the time.

I hold her tightly in the half-lit room. We listen to the rain beating on the roof and the thunder that crashes overhead occasionally. I remember as a child lying in bed and feeling very secure and comfortable in my warm bed with the sounds of the rain outside. Holding Leslie close to me, I feel as content as I did then.

Gently, Leslie kisses me on the lips, then burrows

down within the curve of my arm, her head resting on my shoulder. One finger absently traces circles around my nipple. I turn my head and kiss her forehead.

We hold each other very tightly, as if nothing could tear us apart. From below, we can hear the faint, muffled voices of people in the gallery, but we have no desire to join the outside world right now. For the moment, we are complete, lying together in the bed.

We talk for a long time, punctuating with tiny kisses. She tells me that she has always wanted to visit Disneyworld, and likes the idea of eating vine-ripened tomatoes in the middle of December.

I tell her I am thinking about setting my next book in a seaside town in the dead of winter. She listens carefully. We know we are both telling the truth.

BIRTHDAY GIFTS

Sylvia's birthday was the day after Valentine's Day. I always made sure that there was a little gift for both days, but I always thought she was like a child born on Christmas with her birthday overshadowed. There was always the second present to remind her, and it was impossible to find a quiet restaurant since most were filled with couples around that time. It also seemed strange to receive a Valentine gift from her so close to her birthday. I always felt that she should be the only one receiving presents.

This year, our fifth Valentine's together, I was determined to make two very special days for her to celebrate. Fortunately, they fell on Saturday and

Sunday, and I planned a retreat for both of us from work, the house, and the telephone that always seemed to be ringing off the wall.

I planned the weekend very carefully. I selected three nights at a fine, full-service hotel in the middle of the city. That way, if we didn't want to venture outside in the cold, we could enjoy the pool, the sauna, the first-class restaurant and even some quiet room service. I also made sure it was close to the lively theater strip, and I booked Friday-night tickets for a play along with late-night dinner reservations at Sylvia's favorite Italian restaurant.

Then came the problem of a gift. I didn't have a clue what to buy her, until I sat and read the daily paper. Tucked into a corner, amid all the ads for flower shops and candy stores, was a picture of a gorgeous woman with the address of a store selling sex toys. I immediately knew what Sylvia was going to be unwrapping!

The store wasn't huge, but it was crammed with goodies. I was overwhelmed by the selection—bottles of oil, vibrators in all different sizes and shapes, chrome ben-wah balls, nipple jewelry, lingerie, leather restraints, unusually-shaped candies. I hardly knew where to begin.

Fortunately, the shop owner was more than happy to help. She had several suggestions for a lesbian couple hoping to enjoy a dream weekend, and when I left, I was several dollars lighter, but I had a bag containing a bottle of flavored lotion, a vibrator and a large dildo with a harness.

I surprised Sylvia when she came home from work on Friday afternoon. I gave her a card outlining everything that was planned. I thought she would be excited, but I could never have guessed how much she loved the idea of our special weekend away for two. As excited as two schoolgirls, we packed small suitcases, then got ready to go.

As usual, it didn't work out quite the way we planned. When I came out of the shower, the towel wrapped around me, Sylvia was waiting outside the door. Ever so gently, she kissed me on the lips, then pressed her tongue inside.

The towel dropped as I met her deep kiss. Her hands were on my breasts, kneading and tugging at my erect nipples, and I moaned and reached for her under her shirt. She leaned back and took it off, exposing the beautiful, chocolate-brown tits that I just loved to suck on.

I wasted no time in doing just that. Sylvia groaned as I licked and sucked each one slowly, pulling the nipples out gently between my teeth. Then I led her into the bedroom and helped her off with her skirt and panties.

At her urging I got on top of her, my pussy over her lips, her sweet hole below mine. In seconds we were into a hot sixty-nine. I could have spent all night lapping at her sweet rich cunt, and by the sounds of it, she was certainly having fun giving me the same type of tongue-lashing on my hot, swollen clit.

Sylvia got wetter and hotter the more I drove my tongue into her pussy. I sucked in her juices, licking her from top to bottom with long strokes. She was giving my clit all she had, sending ripples of pleasure through my legs and belly. She knew how to eat pussy, and was giving a wonderful performance.

I matched her motions, sucking and licking her clit. It was tough to do because she was bucking wildly, just as I was. Both of us were in a frenzy, grinding our pussies down onto each other's tongues, trying to lick each other as hard as we could. It felt so good to have her hot tongue between my pussy lips. I knew how good my own tongue must have felt in her cunt.

Even the sounds were turning me on—the moans from both of us, and the wet licking-noises as we ate each other out. I was getting so excited. I seemed to be surrounded everywhere by pussy juice and the beautiful smell of hot sex.

I couldn't help myself. My muscles tightened up and the white-hot sparks moved from my pussy up my spine. As Sylvia pushed her tongue into my cunt, I exploded. Moaning and thrashing my clit on her tongue, I kept my own still on her hot button. Moments later she came, too, pushing up to meet my mouth. She seemed to shiver and come for the longest time.

It also seemed to take the longest time to calm down from our explosive orgasms. It felt so good lying totally relaxed in my Sylvia's arms, and I could have happily stayed that way forever. However, Sylvia was a bit more realistic than I was, and she reminded me that we risked missing the play if we didn't get moving.

We dressed quickly. Sylvia wore my favorite dress, a gorgeous gold silk one that showed off her firm breasts, with a short skirt that let me see her beautiful legs. She spent several hours at the gym each week, and her gorgeous body showed the results. I could look at her for hours. Her thighs were firm, her belly was flat, and her tight skin was flawless. I exercised as well, but I didn't have quite the resolve that Sylvia did. I was fonder of sitting with a book than of pumping iron. Still, the little bit I did kept me in decent shape, and Sylvia loved to run her hands over my slightly rounder curves and softer skin. We were well suited for each other, and loved each other dearly.

Our first stop was the hotel. The doorman held

the taxi door open for us, and it seemed as if we were stepping into another world. The brightly lit façade was all 1920s art deco, and we walked to the huge glass doors along a red carpet that stretched across the sidewalk. Inside, the glorious old building was completely refurbished, and the lobby was an enormous, thickly-carpeted room filled with overstuffed couches and wing chairs. Dark paneling was illuminated by the enormous crystal chandelier that hung from the ceiling several stories above. I felt as if I had stepped into a movie.

Once we had registered, we walked toward the elevator. Sylvia insisted on a quick detour, and soon we were peeking into a thoroughly modern pool and exercise room, much to her delight. I knew I would have at least a couple of hours poolside while she checked out the fitness equipment, and was grateful for the thick book I had tucked into my bag and the bar I saw in the corner.

We went to our room. Like the lobby, it was opulently decorated, with old-fashioned rose wallpaper, mahogany trim, and a huge king-sized bed with thick pillows. The television and tiny refrigerator were hidden inside a huge carved wooden cabinet. The room was finished with a comfortable loveseat, two huge wing chairs, and a small table.

To my delight and Sylvia's surprise, I saw that the hotel had remembered the chilled bottle of champagne I had ordered. It was sitting in a silver ice bucket on the little table, and when we had hung up our clothes, we sat down in the matching wing chairs and poured two glasses.

"A toast to us," I proposed, and Sylvia touched my glass. The champagne slipped down like silk.

"I know it's early," I continued, "but your gift this year is something you might want to open before the end of the weekend." I slipped the brightly-wrapped present out of the corner of my suitcase and placed it before her.

Sylvia smiled. "I have a Valentine's present for you, too," she admitted. "I know it isn't until tomorrow, but this is the kind of gift that you won't want to wait for."

I made her open her present first. The look on her face was worth all of the time spent shopping. She was delighted with the vibrator and the nipple lotion, but was absolutely enthralled with the dildo and harness. Promising that she would make good use of all three before the weekend was over, she urged me to open my gift. She had a knowing smile on her face.

I removed the wrapping paper. Inside, from the same store I had purchased her gifts from, was a double-headed dildo. I was fascinated. I had seen them in the store and was turned on by the idea, but I didn't know if Sylvia would be interested as well. Knowing that she was made me want to forget the play and dinner and try it out right then. I told her how excited I was.

Sylvia smiled and poured another glass of champagne for us. "We'll leave all these toys here and think about them when we're out," she said. "Just imagine how hot we're going to be when we come back."

I reluctantly agreed, and knew that my pussy was going to be throbbing all the time I was out. I did get back at her, though, by reaching over and kissing Sylvia deeply. I then put my hand under her short skirt and rubbed her soft pussy through her thin panties until she closed her eyes and sighed. I could feel her flesh getting hotter and hotter. Just when I could feel her panties start to get moist, I sat back in my chair and concentrated on my champagne. She started to protest, until I reminded her that we were even. She laughed and agreed.

We corked the half-empty bottle of champagne, freshened our makeup, and went downstairs. We decided to walk, since the night wasn't very cold, and because we were early we stopped in a Japanese restaurant for a little something to tide us over until dinner.

Sitting at the sushi bar was almost torture, and the night had only begun. Perched on the small chair, toying with a tiny cup of sake, I could feel my pussy burning as I thought of the presents that were waiting back in the room for us. It was even more difficult every time I looked at her. Her chopsticks slid smoothly between her gorgeous lips, just as my nipples did when she sucked on them. Her graceful hands holding the tiny ceramic sake cup were just as suited to making me come by rubbing on my fiery clit. Under her dress I knew the curve of her breasts, the way her nipples got hard when I touched them. Sylvia was very beautiful and she drew glances from around the sushi bar. I almost felt weak at the knowledge that she belonged to me.

The theater was just as difficult. I concentrated so hard on my throbbing pussy that I barely noticed the plot. When the waiter seated us for our late dinner, I was afraid I was going to go right over the table for Sylvia's beautiful body. She had been right; I was cooking myself into a frenzy, waiting to get back to the hotel to try out our new toys. The food was delicious as always, but I was never so glad to see the check come. Rather than spend time walking back, we hailed a taxi outside the restaurant.

We got on the hotel elevator with another couple, who got off several floors before our own. As soon as the elevator door closed again, Sylvia turned to me and whispered, "I could barely keep my hands off you all night!" Immediately we were locked in a deep kiss, her hand straying up to hold my breast. Finally we were at our floor.

Inside the room, Sylvia played a maddeningly slow game of undressing me. Each button of my dress was undone, and then Sylvia's tongue carefully traced designs on the skin underneath. When my dress was off, she spent several minutes kissing my neck and throat before moving down to unhook my bra. When that was off, she lavished all her attention on my nipples, which were as hard as rocks. I felt weak as she sucked at them and gently nibbled on them with her teeth.

When I was completely naked, it was her turn. I kissed and sucked at every inch of smooth, dark skin I uncovered. When all of her clothes were in a pile on the chair, I made her lie down on the bed and opened the bottle of flavored lotion.

It was thick and creamy on my fingers, and I rubbed it into her nipples. She moaned and told me the lotion was getting hot. I quickly found out, when I bent over to lick her beautiful tits, that indeed it was. A gorgeous warmth flooded my mouth as I took my Sylvia's nipples between my lips.

Sylvia got up and anointed my nipples with the strawberry-flavored liquid. It was a lovely warmth, and even more so when Sylvia lay on her back and instructed me to lean over her face. I could now suck and knead on her breasts while my own hung above her lips. For the longest time we stayed in this mini-sixty-nine, lavishing attention on each other's nipples. Every now and again I would reach down and run my fingers over Sylvia's hot pussy, and she would moan and suck on my nipples until I thought I would almost come.

Getting up, I poured some of the strawberry lotion on my fingers and slowly rubbed it into the lips around Sylvia's pussy, and the insides of her thighs. Soon she was basking in the warmth, and I leaned down and slowly licked the smooth skin of her legs, moving in to her inner thighs and her beautiful pussy. She groaned and begged me to lick her clit, but I kept my achingly slow pace.

I ran my tongue over her pussy lips, breathing hard on her clit and occasionally brushing my tongue lightly over it. Each time she moaned and begged to be eaten. I kept teasing her, then finally began to lick her beautiful cunt.

She let out a loud moan of delight. Her pussy was just as naturally sweet as the strawberry lotion, and I couldn't get enough. I pushed my tongue into her hole and fucked her with it, then rolled her clit between my tongue and my lips. I was so hot myself I reached between my legs and fingered my own pussy. The sight of Sylvia on her back with her legs spread for me, the honey taste of her pussy, her squeals of pleasure were too much for me. I rubbed my clit hard and licked her.

Sylvia held my head, pushing my tongue deep into her pussy. I licked harder and faster, all the time rubbing my own clit hard. My fingers were soaked with my own juices, and my face was wet from Sylvia's nectar. Both of us were moving, pushing our pussies up and down.

We came at almost the same time. It was difficult to lick Sylvia when the hot waves moved through me, but seconds later she cried out and pulled me deep into her cunt.

It was one of the most intense I'd ever had. I collapsed in Sylvia's arms on the huge bed, panting. She was just as weak from hers as I was. We held each other tightly until we both calmed down. It was late, so we slipped under the smooth cotton sheets and switched the bedside light off. The bed was very comfortable and the pillows luxuriously fluffy, and I fell asleep almost immediately.

We were awakened in the morning by a quick rap at the door. It was our breakfast, hot croissants and coffee, with a pot of preserves on the side. I had never felt so pampered before. We opened the curtains and moved the chairs close to the window, so we could watch the city streets below while enjoying our meal. Sylvia was fascinated with the view and as I looked at her profile, holding her cup of coffee while the weak winter sun played on her face, I didn't think I had ever seen her look more beautiful.

When breakfast was finished, I went into the bathroom and prepared for my shower. As with most hotels where I'd stayed, the water pressure wasn't fantastic, but at least it was good and hot. I stepped under the stream and closed my eyes to wet my face.

Suddenly I felt familiar hands on me. Sylvia was in the shower with me, running her fingers up and down my wet body. We kissed under the shower head, the water pouring down our faces and making our kiss even steamier.

The weekend away had turned us both insatiable. Within moments, our hands were in each other's pussies.

Sylvia reached around the shower curtain for the thick terry washcloth. It was a fairly large one, and she soaked it under the shower head, doubled it over, and draped it over her hand. Then she rubbed it between my legs.

Sparks went off. The rough fabric tickled my clit like I'd never felt before. I moaned, and held her tightly to me, kissing her while she rubbed with the cloth. I was so hot my tongue was almost down her throat and I wanted to go even deeper.

Deftly she turned us around so that I was under the shower head. The hot water streamed down my body as Sylvia kissed me, one hand rubbing my nipple, the other sending hot rushes through my pussy with the washcloth.

It didn't take long. I had never come standing up before, and I didn't think I could do it. But the beautiful burning in my pussy quickly spread through my whole body and I cried out. It was so intense I had to get out of the shower; between my orgasm and the hot steamy water, I thought I would faint.

I dried off while Sylvia finished her shower. When she was done, I dried her with the huge, fluffy bath towel. "Now it's your turn," I said, teasing her dark pussy by rubbing gently with the towel. I led her out of the bathroom and made her sit in one of the wing chairs. "It's time to try out your new toy," I said, taking the vibrator out of its box.

It was dildo-shaped, long and thin with a smooth head and ribs down the sides. It made a low buzzing sound when I turned it on, and it had a dial for different speeds. I set it on low, and knelt before my wonderful Sylvia, sitting in the chair with her legs apart, her pussy still moist from the shower.

I started on the insides of her thighs, moving the vibrator closer and closer to her pussy. Still on the low speed, I traced around her hairy lips with the tip. She murmured her approval.

I moved toward her clit, turning the vibrator on higher. She closed her eyes and moved lower in the chair so that I could touch all of her pussy with the humming wand. When I touched her clit she moaned.

I moved it all over her pussy, turning up the dial slowly. She was squirming on the chair, enjoying every second of it. "Put it inside me," she begged, and I spread her beautiful lips with my fingers and gently pressed the tip inside.

Deeper and deeper I pushed it in, then pulled it back. I fucked her with it, rubbing her clit with my finger at the same time. "Faster, please!" she moaned, and I rubbed hard on her hot button while pushing the vibrator deep into her tunnel.

Her orgasm exploded. Thrashing on the chair, she pushed my hand so the vibrator was right inside her. Moaning, crying out, she shivered violently for the longest time. When I finally turned the vibrator off and pulled it out, shiny with her juices, she was slumped in the chair, breathing heavily and smiling at me.

After deciding how we were going to spend our day, we got dressed and went downstairs to walk along the crowded streets and visit some of the interesting shops. We seldom went into that area, and it was like exploring a whole new city. There had been a lot of renovations since our last visit, and most of the old, run-down storefronts had been turned into brand new stores, some of them elegant and expensive, a few quirky and filled with offbeat items. It was fascinating and before we knew it, it was noon. We stopped into a small deli and enjoyed heaping corned beef sandwiches and hot, homemade soup.

Gradually we made our way back to the hotel. Sylvia was eager to try out the exercise room, and we gathered our suits and made our way down to the pool. She changed into her leotards and went off to the huge room. Its glass wall faced the pool and I could see her inside, sweating and puffing as she jogged on the treadmill. I smiled, took a sip from the cold glass of white wine on the little table beside me, and stretched out on the comfy lounge chair with my book.

Still, I couldn't help sneaking glances every now and again over the top of my book. Sylvia tried out all of the equipment, her skin glistening, her muscles taut under her leotard. She was magnificent. At one point, I noticed that a pair of businessmen walking past the pool stopped and watched her as she moved up and down on the stair-climber. I was almost overcome with pride and the knowledge that no matter how much they wanted her, she belonged to me alone. I wondered if they could even imagine everything we did together, the things we had already done in this hotel, and the toys that were waiting upstairs for us.

She stayed in the room for almost an hour and a half. When she was finished, she ducked into the changing room and came out in her bathing suit. Together we entered the empty pool, swimming several laps together. There was a whirlpool bath in the corner and we decided to try it out. Sylvia pressed the switch on the wall and the small, round pool bubbled into life.

The water was very hot, and felt delicious as it cascaded around us. Then I discovered the water jets! Situated around the pool walls were the jets where the pressurized water flowed in. We quickly discovered that if we faced them and bent our knees, the rush of water, as hard as the touch of a hand, would tickle our pussies! We stayed in the whirlpool for half an hour, enjoying the teasing rush of water on our cunts. We giggled like children when we saw hotel guests walking by the glass-walled pool—if they only knew we were turning ourselves on!

Finally the timer on the whirlpool clicked off, and the bubbling stopped. We swam a few more laps in the pool to refresh ourselves, then changed and went back upstairs, our pussies still tingling from the mad rush of steamy hot water.

We had decided that it would be too crowded in the hotel's dining room, since it was Valentine's Day, and a quick peek inside proved us right. Fortunately we had already placed our order for room service, and we had scarcely dried our hair and changed into silk lounging pajamas before we heard the knock at the door.

I could not recall a better Valentine's dinner. Again we placed our chairs before the window, but now the view was almost magical, with the lights of the city spread out before us. We enjoyed a long, romantic kiss at the window before sitting down to our meal. A perfectly-cooked chateaubriand, baby vegetables, and hot rolls were waiting for us under the silver serving bells, along with a bottle of wine.

Dinner took a long time, what with us lingering over the food and discussing our day. When it was finished, though, it was time for dessert, and Sylvia eagerly brought it over: the box containing the dildo and harness.

Neither of us had used such a device before, and were very intrigued by it. As always, we started with long, slow, deep kisses, and caressing each other's bodies, hers the firm, hard one of an athlete, mine softer and yielding to her lovely touch.

Sylvia spread out on the huge bed. I strapped the harness on. The dildo stood out, large and veined, from my mound. It looked unusual but very interesting, and we both played with it for a while.

I licked Sylvia's pussy until her flesh was hot and moist, delicious as always. Then I lightly coated the dildo with jelly, and pressed its head to the opening between her chocolate lips.

Lying over her, I pushed my hips in and the dildo slid into her. She gasped. I loved the feeling of hovering over her, pushing the rubber head in and out. It didn't take long for me to work up a regular rhythm, pumping the dildo into her.

It turned me on to pump my hips that way, to fill her up. I kissed her while I stroked the dildo inside her. She moved her hand down between us and rubbed her hard clit while I fucked her. My own pussy was throbbing and I reached back to touch myself.

Moaning, gasping, we made love, the dildo going in and out of her soaked pussy, both of us rubbing our clits as hard as we could. I slowed down and gave her long, luscious strokes, then pumped hard and fast into her. She groaned and begged for my kiss. I felt as if I could come into her right through the dildo, I was so hot.

"Let's change positions," Sylvia suggested, and I pulled the wet shaft out. It was my turn to lie flat on the bed. The dildo stuck straight up, its head shiny with pussy juice. The harness was soaked with honey from both of us.

Sylvia got over me and straddled it. Ever so slowly, she sank down on it, until her pussy was resting on me. Soon she was bouncing up and down on it, pushing me into the soft bed, her beautiful tits moving with her rhythm. I played with her nipples, pulling at them and tweaking them between my fingers while she fucked me.

She played with her clit while she moved on the dildo. I couldn't believe how gorgeous she looked, grinding her hips on me, my hands on her breasts, her fingers rubbing her hot clit. Finally it was too much and she came violently, the dildo pushed into her cunt, her hand moving hard on her pussy. I was sure the guests in the next room could hear her, she cried out so much.

In an instant she was off me, unbuckling the harness and pulling the dildo away. Then she leaned down and pressed her mouth to my pussy. Her tongue moved furiously on my clit and before I knew it, I was coming too, crying out just as she had.

Once again we found ourselves in each other's arms, quivering from the passion we had just shared. The dildo and its harness lay on the corner of the bed, and we knew that this was one toy that was not going to be thrown in the drawer and forgotten. Anything that could make us feel that good was going to get its fair share of use.

Eventually we both showered and dressed, then went down to the dining room. At that late hour it was almost deserted, and we picked a cozy table in the corner. It was time for our second dessert, and this time we enjoyed rich coffee and almost sinful chocolate cheesecake. If nothing else, this was going to be our weekend to spoil ourselves silly, and never mind the cost or the calories. On the way back to the room we found that the bar was in full swing, with a band playing on the stage, so we stopped inside for "just one drink" and ended up staying until two.

Sylvia's birthday dawned cold and rainy, and after breakfast in the dining room we got a taxi and went to the museum. Both of us enjoyed the visit, but in the back of my mind all I could see was Sylvia naked before me on the bed, her beautiful body waiting for my touch. She must have felt the same way, too, for whenever we were in an empty hall she would mischievously brush against my breasts or quickly run a hand over my pussy. I longed to be back in our room, and when we had seen everything in the museum, I happily hailed a cab and gave the driver the name of the hotel.

This time we didn't even think about dinner. We

still had one more toy to play with, the double-ended dildo that Sylvia had given to me. It was daylight when we got back to our room, but I knew it would be dark before I would be finished making love with her.

It was a fair-sized one, almost as big as the one I had fucked her with, but with a smooth head at each end. We played at coating it with lubricant, stroking its length and rubbing the crease under the head. Sylvia stretched out on the bed and I caressed her pussy with my fingers, brushing her clit and stroking the lips. Gently I inserted my finger into her hole. Her soft well walls opened for me and held my finger with its velvety muscles. Then I pushed the dildo into her.

The second head and its long shaft stuck out of her, and I wanted to be on it and as close to her as I could be. I eased it into my own pussy, until our cunts met, the dildo deep inside both of us.

I felt wonderfully full, and at the same time teased as Sylvia's hair brushed against my clit. Slowly we began to move on the dildo, to fuck both ourselves and each other. It was difficult at first, but we quickly picked up a rhythm. Soon our pussies were rubbing against each other, the dildo sunk deep in our cunts.

Sylvia reached over and grabbed the vibrator, which we had left on the bedside table. (Who knows what the maid was thinking!) She switched it on and put it between us, so that each time we moved on the dildo, our clits pushed against the humming, vibrating wand.

It felt too good. I stopped pumping on the dildo and pushed against the vibrator. This pressed it tightly against Sylvia's clit, and we squirmed against it, bodies touching, cunts filled with the dildo, clits grinding against the buzzing vibrator.

Moaning, gasping, crying out with pleasure, we rubbed on the vibrator as hard as we could. I came, my eyes closed, shouting. She exploded also, pulling the vibrator as tightly as she could into her hot flesh, trembling and wetting both the vibrator and me with her juices.

I hardly had the strength to move. Sylvia hugged me tightly, the double dildo lying beside us on the bed, the vibrator forgotten and fallen to the floor. We kissed deeply. Sylvia told me that the weekend had been a dream present, the best birthday she had ever spent.

I had planned for us to go to work directly from the hotel in the morning. Sylvia snuggled into my arms and said that she wished the weekend would never end.

I held her close, and we thought about what to have for dinner, and what excuses we would give to our bosses on Monday morning when we called in sick.

METER MAID

It sure wasn't much of a night, I thought, as I waited for the traffic light to change. No one standing on the streets, no orders on the radio. I turned the cab around the corner and slowly cruised down the street. Nothing.

The dispatcher called for a car close to an intersection a few blocks away from where I was. I grabbed the microphone quickly and told him my location. It took a few tries to get through, since a lot of other drivers were trying for it too. I was beaten by a car two blocks closer than I was. Nobody was making any money tonight, and they were fighting furiously over the few calls that came in. I might have been better off staying home.

I decided to go and sit at the nearest cab stand and hope that someone would come along. There was already another car there, but it was better than driving around burning my gas. I pulled in and parked behind it.

I turned the car off and slumped in the seat, sipping my cup of take-out coffee and listening to the cab radio. There was a small flurry of three orders, none of them even close to me, then silence. I hoped I was going to make enough to be able to fill the tank with gas when my shift was over.

I watched as a gorgeous, well-dressed woman walked along the sidewalk. She looked into the cab ahead of me, then walked toward my car. I could see her looking at me directly. Then she motioned to ask if my car was available. I nodded, and sat up straight, putting the coffee cup in its holder.

The driver up ahead had been watching her in his rearview mirror. When she reached for the door handle, he jumped out of his car. "Hey, lady!" he shouted. "I'm the first car at the stand. You have to take my car!"

My passenger didn't seem the least bit ruffled as she opened the rear door. "I'm the one paying the fare," she said. "I can take any car I want, and I want this one." He glared at her, then got back behind the wheel and slammed the door shut angrily.

She gave me an address, a condominium apartment building almost on the other side of the city. Maybe the evening wasn't going to be a total write-off after all. It would be a pretty hefty fare.

I pulled out onto the street and turned the meter on. I wondered why she had chosen my car over the one in front of me at the cab stand. They were both the same model, both in the same condition and both just as clean. For a moment I entertained the thought that maybe she preferred women, but dropped it just as quickly. I knew I couldn't be that lucky.

I stopped for a red light, and looked at her in the rearview mirror. She was the type of woman I often dreamed about. Her clothes were beautiful and expensive-looking, and her hair was carefully arranged. Her face had a model's finely-cut features and beautifully drawn lips that I could just imagine kissing.

She looked up and caught my eyes in the mirror. She smiled. I thought it looked inviting, but I couldn't be sure. The light changed and I started up again.

"You don't see a lot of women driving at night," she said. Her voice was soft and elegant, but I decided not to get my hopes up. It was too good to be true; that sort of thing only happened in stories.

"I've always preferred the night shift," I said. "I don't have to haul a lot of grocery bags, and the money's better. Except on nice nights like this. Most people walk or take the bus. They don't want to spend the money for a cab."

"I was thinking about the bus," she said. "But then I saw you sitting there and decided I really didn't want to wait for one."

"Why didn't you take the first car?"

Again I caught her eye in the mirror, and she smiled. "Your car looked much more interesting."

"Why do you say that?" I asked, curious.

"I prefer women drivers," she said.

My mind was racing, and now I felt my pussy starting to stir. A lot of people say that, but they were referring to the way I handled the car. I didn't really believe that was her intention, although it was lovely to think it was. I began to feel warm, and turned the air conditioning up a notch. Glancing in the mirror, I saw that my gorgeous passenger looked as cool and calm as could be.

"Are you married?" she asked suddenly.

"Oh, no," I replied quickly. How could I explain that my love was reserved for women? That I loved to suck on female nipples, to probe clits with my tongue and smell the beautiful aroma of a woman's soft flesh? "I—I'm not really the type to have a husband," I said, and hoped desperately that she would catch the implication.

"I know what you mean," she said. "I've never been drawn toward it either."

Now my mind was really moving. I squirmed in the seat to relieve some of the pressure on my pussy. I had to be right! Every time I looked in the rearview mirror, I seemed to catch her eye.

It didn't take long to reach her address once I was on the highway. My heart sank a little when I turned off at her exit and her building was in sight. I really didn't want her to leave my cab.

I pulled up at the front door, put the meter on hold, and turned on the interior light so I could write the address on the trip sheet that I had to fill out after every passenger. Again she looked in the mirror, and I glanced at her and admired her as she opened her purse and looked for her wallet. I could still feel the quick thrill I got when our eyes met.

"Oh, dear," she said, looking in her wallet. "I thought I had another twenty. I'm a bit short." I groaned to myself, and realized that her tone sounded as if she was reciting a practiced speech. Still, it didn't add up. Deadbeats didn't usually live in classy buildings and wear expensive clothes.

"You can park the car over there and come upstairs with me to get the money," she said, indicating the nearby visitor parking lot. "I have more upstairs. I just forgot to bring it with me."

Normally my rule was never to go into a building
with a passenger, for my own safety. But this time my
throbbing pussy overruled my better judgment. True,
I did want the money. Even more, though, I wanted
to keep this fascinating woman in my sight, if only for
a few extra minutes.

I let the dispatcher know that I wouldn't be
answering the radio for a short time, then parked the
car and followed her to the front door of the building. As we went up in the elevator, the sensual smell
of her perfume reached me and I wanted her so
badly I couldn't believe it.

She opened the door to her apartment, which was
large and beautifully decorated. She closed and
locked it behind us, and then turned to face me. I felt
like I was in a crazy dream when she reached up and
stroked my cheek with her fingertips. "You told me it
was a really slow night," she said. "Do you have to go
back out so soon?"

My heart was racing as I realized that I was going
to get exactly what I had wanted. Her touch was soft
but as hot as a flame to me. She ran her fingernails
down my neck and then stopped just above the top
button of my shirt, tracing a tiny design back and
forth on my skin.

"You want this as much as I do, don't you?" she
asked.

"Yes," I whispered, and she kissed me. Her lips
were warm and sweet. She grew bolder and I felt her
tongue press into my mouth. My pussy was so hot I
wanted desperately to touch it and control the throbbing. I pushed my own tongue against hers, and I felt
her moan softly as I did.

As I kissed her, I could feel her hands unbuttoning
my shirt. When it was open, she reached inside. I
wasn't wearing a bra and her hands were warm and

smooth on my tits. She never stopped kissing me, and her hands kept moving over my skin.

I could feel my nipples get hard and tingly. She brushed them gently, then held them between her fingers and pressed them firmly. I moaned and put my arms around her.

She broke away and took my hand. "There's plenty of time," she said. "We don't have to do everything in the hallway." She led me to her bedroom. The focal point was a large bed with the head and foot fashioned out of black wrought iron and decorated with metal vines and grape leaves. It was covered with a thick, ivory-colored duvet.

"Please undress me," she said. I was only too eager to. She was wearing a tailored suit, and I slipped the blazer off her shoulders. Then I unbuttoned her silk blouse, revealing a lacy black bra under it.

I couldn't wait another minute. Her nipples were pointing out against the fabric, and I took them into my mouth. I nibbled them right through the bra. She groaned and held my head while I sucked at them. Then I reached carefully into one cup and pulled her large tit out. Her nipple was huge, with a large brown areola studded with tiny goosebumps surrounding it. I licked and sucked it into my mouth. Her skin tasted warm and rich and I took as much of her into my mouth as I could. I could feel her quiver just a little when I pulled back and pushed my tongue against the very tip of her nipple. I blew on it to cool it, then sucked it back into my warm mouth and she moaned again.

I reached behind her and unhooked the bra, then took it off her completely. Her breasts were lovely. I pushed them together and ran my tongue over both of her nipples, back and forth. I licked in between them and pushed them against my cheeks. I wanted to bury myself in them, they were so large and warm.

"Don't stop there," she said, and I reached for the small zipper on her skirt. When it dropped to the floor I discovered that she wasn't wearing any panties, but her stockings were held up with black garters decorated with tiny red silk roses. The garters looked delicious, and framed her dark triangle superbly.

"Let me lie down," she begged. The black garters looked even better against the light duvet. "Now, come here." My shirt hanging open, my jeans still on, I climbed onto the bed. She motioned for me to kiss her, and I did gladly. She massaged my tits while my mouth was on hers. I put my hand between her legs.

Her pussy was damp and slippery, and burning hot to my fingers. I moved up and down her fleshy, hairy lips, then gently pushed them apart. Her clit was huge. She pushed her tongue passionately into my mouth when I touched it, and her hands moved even faster on my tits. I wondered how crazy she would go once my tongue was on it, and I longed to lick it.

I moved my hand back to explore her hole. It felt so good to put my finger up inside her and feel the velvet-soft muscles grab and hold me tight. I moved in and out of it slowly. I loved to pull my finger out until it was almost free, then move it with short strokes and finally bury it again right up to my hand. She liked it and when I pushed in deeply, she moved her hips to grind against me and fill herself with my probing finger.

I wanted to taste her cunt so badly. I worked my way down her body slowly, licking and kissing her as I went. I dipped my tongue into the little indentation at the base of her throat, and from there moved down to her tits, licking and kissing each one a few times. I swept down her flat belly in long sweeps of my tongue and finally found myself at her beautiful pussy.

I licked all over her pussy lips and then stabbed at her clit with my tongue. She went wild, just as I thought she would. She moaned and gasped, then told me how good it felt. I loved to hear her and it spurred me on to lick faster.

"Lick me there," she said. "Right there on my hard clit! Ooh, just to the side, now harder, faster, right where you're licking. I love having my cunt lapped like that!"

I licked my finger and rubbed the entrance to her hole while I moved my tongue all over her clit. Her pussy tasted like ruby red wine, so delicious that I wanted to lick up every drop of her juice.

"That's so warm, so good!" she moaned, and she put her hands on my head and pulled me in so that my tongue pushed hard against her clit. "Oh, you lick pussy so well. Lick me again right there. Keep your finger on my hole!"

I was going crazy on her cunt now. She squeezed me between her thighs, and the soft sheer stockings slid, whisper-smooth, against my cheeks. I couldn't move, couldn't leave her pussy, and I didn't want to. Her juice was everywhere, on my chin and lips and on her thighs. I was surrounded completely by her cunt.

I licked her every way I knew possible. I tickled her clit with just the knife-edge tip of my tongue, and lapped her whole cunt with my tongue stretched out wide and flat. I pushed her clit back and forth and sucked it between my lips, flicking over it and nibbling on it gently with my teeth. All the time I was doing this, she was murmuring to me, telling me when I was hitting sensitive spots and when I should speed up or slow down. Her voice was as smooth as oiled silk and I loved to hear her.

My tongue hit a spot that she really enjoyed and I stayed on it, using short strokes to brush against it. Her voice got louder and she moaned. I kept at it, and she came.

She almost screamed as she did, and she bounced her pussy up and down on my tongue. Her cunt was all over my face and I reveled in it. She was so wild and excited I couldn't believe it was the same cool, elegant woman who sat so straight in my cab. I had never been with anyone so enthusiastic. I was so turned on that, my own pussy was crying out for immediate attention.

"Come up here," she gasped, and she kissed me hard and licked her own pussy nectar off my face. Then she unzipped my jeans and helped me to get them off. She got up and made me sit on the edge of the bed, then slipped my shirt off my shoulders and tossed it aside.

She knelt before me on the thick carpeting and took my tits into her mouth. Her tongue was as hot as her pussy and I groaned as she licked my nipples hard.

"Feels good, doesn't it?" she asked, and I could only nod. Her hand was on my thigh, moving up and down by my steamy cunt. "Your tits are so nice, I could suck on them for hours. But I want to taste your pretty pussy too."

She moved down so that her head was between my open legs. The first touch of her hot tongue on my clit was electric. My pussy was soaked and she licked my juice away first. "You taste so good," she said. "I knew you would as soon as I saw you. I knew you would want your cunt eaten."

She was doing a beautiful job. Her experienced tongue sought the folds of my pussy and moved up and down the sides of my clit. I forced myself to calm down. I didn't want to come quickly. I wanted to keep her tongue on my clit, building me up, as long as I possibly could. It just felt so wonderful and I wanted to draw it out.

It was as if she had read my mind, for she left my clit and licked my thighs slowly. I breathed out hard and relaxed, but just as I did, she pushed her tongue against my clit again. The white-hot shivers went up and down my spine, and my whole body was once again concentrated on that small nub of flesh that she was going crazy over.

She moved down to tongue my hole and then suddenly I realized that her wet finger was probing my ass. I leaned back a bit, and she expertly pushed the tip in as smoothly and gently as I could imagine. She wiggled her finger back and forth and I almost came right then and there. I loved the feeling of being full, and the way she licked me made it even better.

I could feel the familiar tingling in my belly and my legs felt weak. My muscles tightened, and she looked up at me and smiled. She licked two fingers on her other hand and pushed them into my pussy hole, then bent forward and licked hard right on my clit.

Wow! Both my holes were filled and my clit was getting a spectacular workout. Within a few moments I was gasping and moaning uncontrollably. There was nothing but the sensation in my pussy; I was aware of nothing else. Everything was forgotten except for those fingers in my ass and my hole, and that hot, wild tongue licking my clit.

I came so hard I made as much noise as she had. My whole body jerked with the wave that went through me. Even my toes and fingertips tingled. I fell back on the bed, and felt so good that I thought all my bones had melted. I didn't have the strength left to raise my hand.

I felt her pull her finger out of my ass. I raised my head and watched as she took her fingers out of my pussy, then put them in her mouth and sucked the syrup from my hole off of them. I had never seen anyone do that before and it turned me on more than I could have imagined it would.

She got onto the bed and stretched out with her head beside me. She kissed me on the lips and pushed the hair back from my damp forehead. "Better than spending your night sitting at a cab stand?" she asked.

"Much," I gasped, and took her face in my hands to kiss her deeply. I hadn't made love like that in ages and I didn't think I'd ever had an orgasm that intense in all my life. She was very, very good and I knew I would remember this session for a long time.

She looked at her watch. "I hate to break up a party," she said, "but I have to meet someone. I have enough money now. Will you take me?"

"Anywhere," I said, and kissed her again. We held each other for a long time, and then got up. Reluctantly I pulled my jeans and shirt back on. I wished I could have slept in her arms the whole night.

We took the elevator back down to where the car was waiting. She sat in the front seat this time, and gave me the address of a restaurant. I had expected her to be chatty and maybe even talk about what we had just done, but even though she was sitting beside me this time, she wasn't any more talkative than on the trip to her apartment. I felt like I was blabbering when I spoke to her, and finally just kept quiet myself and drove.

I pulled up in front of the restaurant, and she took some money out of her purse and pressed it into my palm. I didn't look at it.

She leaned close to me and touched my cheek.

"Don't get me wrong," she said. "I just don't talk much after I'm with someone. It doesn't mean anything. I think you're really great."

She kissed me deeply and pushed the tip of her tongue into my mouth. "You were fantastic," she said. "I hope I meet up with you again soon."

She got out of the cab and disappeared into the bustling restaurant. I looked at the money. She had paid what she owed for the first ride, along with the fare for this trip and a hefty tip on top of it all.

I marked the run on my trip sheet. I sat for a long time at the curb, until the cab radio finally squawked and woke me out of my daydream. I still had five hours to go on my shift. I hoped they would pass quickly. Already I wanted to go home and think about her, and maybe let my hand stray down to my hot pussy while I did.

I put the car in gear and pulled out from the curb. The streets were still empty and I cruised slowly, my eyes checking both sides of the street for people flagging me down.

I turned the corner and headed back to the cab stand, and suddenly remembered that I didn't even know her name.

OPEN CURTAINS

S ummer hit the city particularly hard that year. Throughout the day, the relentless sun beat down until it was possible to feel the heat of the pavement right through a pair of shoes. The late afternoon improved somewhat, but the nights were still steamy. The air was heavy enough that you felt it on your skin when you moved through it.

Sandra sat on her apartment balcony, enjoying her Saturday night. Her long hair was pulled back in a ponytail and she wore only a flimsy white cotton dress. Normally billowy and loose, it clung to her skin, outlining her beautiful breasts and hinting at the dark triangle between her long legs. The can of soda, icy-cold out of the refrigerator, was now only cool. She pressed it to her cheek.

She had only been in the city for a couple of weeks, brought out by a job transfer. Normally she would have been out exploring her new surroundings, but it was just too hot to move and she was satisfied to sit out the sultry night on her tiny balcony. Occasionally she read bits of the magazine on the table beside her. It was so hot even the insects were drowsy, and she could leave the light on without being bothered by them.

Despite the heat, there was plenty of activity both in her own apartment building and the one she faced. Several residents—Sandra not among them—were fortunate enough to have air conditioners, and their hum provided a lazy background noise. One apartment was host to a party, and the music and laughter wafted over to Sandra's balcony. The couple directly below her were also sitting outside, and she could hear their voices. Occasionally a car or a bus would drive along the road that the buildings fronted on. A couple of children, their bedtimes long past, still played on the grass several floors below her. She could even hear the faint hum of machines from the laundry room, although it was beyond her to imagine anyone sitting in the room that the superintendent told her was stifling hot even on the coldest days of winter.

She took a long drink of her soda, then leaned over the balcony railing and looked into the apartments across the way. It was easy to do, since most of them had their lights on and their curtains pulled open. One family was sitting watching television. One group was sitting around the kitchen table playing cards, beer bottles in front of them. And then, directly opposite her and one floor down, she saw something that made her stop and stare.

Two women were standing together in their living room, running their hands through each other's hair and kissing passionately. Everything else was forgotten as Sandra watched, open-mouthed.

They were both lightly dressed and their hands strayed as they kissed. One was taller, light-haired, wearing shorts and a thin T-shirt. The other was darker, and she wore a loose dress similar to Sandra's. As Sandra watched, amazed and fascinated, the blonde lifted the hem of the skirt and put her hand underneath it. By the way the brunette moved, Sandra knew that she was having her pussy felt.

Sandra couldn't believe it. One of her major problems in moving to the new city was being lesbian and not knowing any others. Now they were coming to her!

The pair seemed completely oblivious to the fact that their curtains were open and they could be seen. The brunette lifted her partner's T-shirt. The blonde was not wearing a bra and her breasts were small and firm. The brunette leaned down and took one of them into her mouth. Their apartment had an air conditioner humming in the window. Sandra could just imagine how cool her flesh would feel on this scorching night, and how hard that pink nipple would feel to the lips that held it and the tongue that was licking its tip.

The brunette lavished attention on both of her lover's nipples. Sandra's own mouth opened slightly and her tongue darted out, as if she was the one licking the nude woman. Her pussy was already starting to throb as she watched the blonde close her eyes and give herself over to her partner's caress.

Sandra watched as the tall blonde woman deftly slipped out of her blue shorts. She was not wearing any panties and the brunette's hands were between her legs immediately. Sandra could almost feel the hot blonde pussy lips that the darker woman was caressing with her fingers. Her own hand was on her pussy now through her dress. She played with herself absently as she watched the two women in the apartment. She didn't even care that she was sitting out in the open herself on the balcony.

It was the brunette's turn. She lifted the loose dress over her head and stood before her lover naked. Her breasts were much larger, and Sandra longed to hold them. She watched as the two played with each other's nipples, pausing for deep kisses.

They were all over each other now. Hands were in pussies, lips were on nipples. Sandra marveled at how gorgeous they looked. It was like watching a hot video except that these were real women making love right in front of her eyes. She was so turned on it was frightening. The heat, the noise from her neighbors, everything was forgotten as she stared into the window at the two women who were making love so openly. It almost seemed as if they were putting on a show just for her.

Suddenly the women walked out of the room. Sandra was crushed; she never thought about that happening. Then she noticed that all of the curtains in the apartment were open, and all of the lights were on. She rushed into the living room, but could see nothing. She hurried into the bedroom without turning on her own light.

Perfect! Their bedroom was almost directly across from hers, but one floor lower. She could see almost everything in the room, but especially the bed where the two lovers were now sitting.

They were facing Sandra, who sat on her own bed, close to the window in her darkened bedroom. Again they kissed slowly and sensuously, the blonde's hand rubbing the dark pussy beside her and the brunette running her fingers over her lover's small, firm breasts. They were so perfectly positioned they must have known they were putting on a show. Sandra's dress was pushed up to her hips. Her hand was once again in her hot wet pussy. Her other hand was kneading her breast, her fingers rolling over the nipple under the light cotton dress.

Gently the brunette eased her partner down on the bed until she was on her back, with her legs still over the edge. Sandra could see the blonde pussy and she longed to be near it. The brunette knelt on the carpet and pressed her lips against the waiting pussy.

Sandra gasped. She could almost feel that mouth on her own steamy cunt. She could see the dark head moving and knew the fantastic tongue-lashing that the blonde was receiving. How she longed to be on the receiving end of that attention! Her own hand was now rubbing her clit hard.

The blonde was obviously enjoying her pussy workout. Her hands were on her lover's head to push her tongue deeper in. Sandra could see her mouth open in a moan of pleasure, the same type that escaped from Sandra's lips as her fingers touched her own wet pussy.

The blonde said something, and the brunette stopped and stood up. The blonde moved so that she was lying flat on the large bed. Sandra smiled as she watched the brunette straddle her on the bed, getting ready for some sixty-nine.

They were both hungry for pussy, for they were eating each other out within seconds. Sandra still couldn't believe that she was actually sitting in her bedroom watching them. They were both licking furiously, their hips moving and their pussies grinding on each other's mouths. Sandra's hand was soaked with her own pussy juices. She wanted to be part of them.

The two were giving it everything they had. Sandra saw that the blonde woman was going wild, her hips grinding furiously. Sandra pushed her hand hard against her clit and she came just as the blonde woman did. Both of them trembled as the hot sparks moved through their bodies from their wet cunts. The brunette seemed to explode a few moments later. Sandra could see her mouth open as she cried out with the feeling.

All three of them relaxed. Sandra slumped on the bed. Her pussy felt alive and fantastic and she panted for breath in the stifling air. The two women in their air-conditioned apartment held each other tightly, the brunette moving on the bed so that she could hug her lover and kiss her gently.

They stayed together on the bed for a long time, and Sandra's eyes never left them. Their bodies were beautiful. They talked to each other, kissing every so often and running their hands up and down one another. Sandra was lonely and longed for their company, if only just to sit and talk.

Eventually they got up and dressed, still not caring that their curtains were open. They both put on light summer dresses with no underwear, then fixed their hair and turned the light off. Disappointed, Sandra watched them walk through their living room and go out the front door. The apartment went dark as the blonde hit the light switch on her way out.

Sandra sat in her dark bedroom, her mind replaying their wild, abandoned sex scene. They must have known that people in Sandra's building could see them, but they didn't seem to care. Were they turned on knowing that someone might be watching? More importantly, would they make love in front of the open window again? Sandra certainly hoped so; it was so exciting watching them. After a while, she peeled off her damp dress and dropped it on the floor, then stretched naked on top of the sheets and fell into a deep, satisfied sleep.

All day Sunday she kept an eye on the apartment. The curtains were still open, but in daylight it was impossible to see inside. She sat in her chair on the balcony for almost the entire afternoon, reading a book and glancing up regularly at the apartment windows. The weather was still oppressively hot, but Sandra kept vigil at her outside post.

She was rewarded once. As she watched, the brunette walked to the window where the air conditioner was. Sandra could see her very clearly. Her features were fine, her dark curls falling to her shoulders. After she had adjusted the machine, she stood in front of the window, leaning on the sill and looking out. For a moment she looked at Sandra, who was sitting forward with her arms on the balcony. It seemed as if she flashed a smile right at her. Sandra smiled back. The woman kept looking around, then walked back in the room where Sandra could not see her.

It seemed to take forever for the sun to go down. When it finally did, the lights in the apartment went on, and Sandra could see into their living room. The blonde woman sat in a chair with her back to the window, reading the newspaper. She lifted her head and spoke to someone Sandra couldn't see, then got up. Her heart sinking, Sandra watched her pull the curtains.

She felt terrible. Obviously they had realized what they had done, and were now protecting themselves against prying eyes. She went for a walk down to the small restaurant on the corner where she had some dinner, then came back to her apartment. It seemed even tinier and more stifling. The curtains were still drawn across the way, even the ones in the bedroom. She could see that the lights were on behind them, which made her even more depressed. She wondered just what was going on in that bedroom, on that large inviting bed.

She went to work Monday, but her mind wasn't really on her job. All throughout the day she pictured the two women making love on the bed, over and over. She managed to work herself into such a frenzy that she finally excused herself and went to the washroom. There she rubbed her pussy hard until the soft waves of orgasm rushed up her spine. The rest of the day she wondered if the curtains would ever be opened again on that beautiful couple that turned her on so much.

The curtains stayed closed that night, and the next. Perhaps they had realized their error, or had received a complaint. She had given up hope of ever seeing them again, and on Wednesday night she rode out the heat wave by sitting reading on her balcony. She finished the book late into the night and was just about to go inside when her eyes strayed to the apartment.

The curtains were open. Hardly believing her luck, Sandra sat back down and turned out the little light beside her. The blonde woman was sitting in her chair, her back to Sandra and once again reading a newspaper. Sandra watched her for quite a while. Then the brunette walked into view, took the newspaper away, and leaned down to kiss the blonde woman on the lips.

Sandra was elated, but tried not to get her hopes up too high. She was afraid they would stop and close the curtains, but they didn't. Instead, the brunette eased herself into the blonde's lap and they wrapped their arms around each other, their mouths glued together in long slow kisses.

Sandra longed to be with them in the big chair. Their kisses became more passionate and their hands moved skillfully to caress sensitive areas. It was difficult for Sandra to see all that was going on, since the chair was not facing her, but every now and again she glimpsed the blonde woman's hands massaging her lover's full, large breasts through the flimsy shirt she wore.

Eventually they became too turned on for the confines of the chair. Once again they moved into the bedroom. Sandra followed them into hers. As before, they left the lights on and, to Sandra's joy, the curtains open.

Taking a deep breath, Sandra decided on a plan of action. Normally she was almost painfully shy, but she decided to throw caution to the winds. This moment was just too important to pass up and she might never have the chance again. She turned on her own bedroom light and stood right at the window. From here she could stare down into the bedroom where the two women were now slowly undressing each other.

More importantly, if they looked up through their own window, they would be able to see her standing there watching them. They would only be able to see her from the waist up, but Sandra felt that it would be enough. If they enjoyed being watched and were only doing it to attract attention, seeing her looking at them might be enough to convince them to keep their curtains open all the time. She figured at any rate she had nothing to lose.

She wasn't sure, but she thought she saw the blonde woman glance in her direction before she settled down to licking and sucking her lover's nipples.

The brunette woman was stretched out on the bed, and the blonde licked her with long, slow strokes as if she were made of candy. She pushed the brunette's large breasts together and sucked both nipples into her mouth at once, then concentrated on each one separately as her hand strayed down to the dark pubic hair.

Sandra's hands were on her breasts. They felt soft and full under her shirt, just as the brunette's must have felt under that experienced tongue. She knew that other people would be able to see her as she stood in her brightly lit window, but she was so hot and horny she didn't care. All that mattered were the two women below her, and the pussy that was aching so badly she had to put her hand there. She was burning right through her shorts, and she could feel the wetness of her cunt soaking into the fabric.

The women on the bed were now sitting opposite each other, their legs crossed over so that they were close together. They were caressing each other's breasts slowly and gently, working themselves up. It was effective; Sandra was already close to a fever pitch herself watching them.

Eventually their hands moved down to each other's pussies. Sitting so close together, they were able to kiss each other eagerly. Meanwhile, each had her hand on the other's cunt, rubbing and stroking the hot, hard clit.

Sandra's hand was also firmly on her own clit. Rubbing herself felt so good as she watched the scene being played out in front of her. The two women were obviously enjoying themselves as well. She could see their mouths open in gasps and moans when they weren't kissing each other's mouths, necks, and shoulders.

A heavy warmth was building in Sandra's belly as

she watched the two in the apartment below fucking each other with their hands. The brunette woman came first, throwing her head back, her mouth open and crying out with the force of her orgasm. She kept massaging the blonde's hot wet pussy until the taller woman came as well. Sandra watched her tremble and push her partner's hand into herself, grinding her pussy against it. Then Sandra let herself go and her own explosive orgasm overcame her as she stood by the open window.

Once again she thought she saw the blonde woman glance up at her. The two were now lying in each other's arms on top of the sheets, talking and kissing. Sandra kept standing by the window until the brunette reached over and turned out the light. Satisfied by her orgasm and by watching the couple, she realized how very tired she was. She undressed and lay down on her bed. Although the night was still very hot, she fell asleep almost immediately.

She went off to work again with the two women on her mind. The scene of them rubbing each other kept running through her head like a movie repeated over and over, but each showing was just as hot and exciting as the last. The day seemed to drag along; when she thought she'd been working for an hour, Sandra would look up at the clock and see that only ten minutes had passed. All she wanted to do was rush home and stand by the window in the hopes of catching a glimpse of the two women. Finally it was time to leave, and she rushed out of the building and down to the bus stop. Even though the bus was packed with people and horribly hot, it was a joy for her to ride home.

As her stop came up, she inched her way toward the door through the throng of passengers and got off. After the air in the bus, the hot sun was almost refreshing. She walked to the front door of her building, fumbling for the tiny key that opened her mailbox.

She checked it every day, even though she had moved so recently there hadn't been any mail for her yet. Today was different, though. Tucked amidst the advertising flyers was a small sealed envelope with no name or address written on the front.

She wondered how it could have arrived, until she noticed that there was a crease along the top edge. Someone had folded it and slipped it through the crack at the top of the mailbox door.

She got on the elevator and opened the envelope on her way up. The contents so surprised her that she got off at her floor and just stood in the middle of the hallway so that people had to walk around her to get on the elevator. The handwriting on the blank card was small and neat.

"We know you are watching us," the note read. "Are you one of us? We really hope that you are, and we would like to meet you. If you are interested, we will be at the address below after seven this evening. We would love to meet you." The address was written at the bottom. There were no names on the card, or a return address, but the stationery was heavy and very expensive.

Sandra's heart was beating so hard her hands were trembling. She could barely fit the key into her apartment door. She rushed over to the window, but the curtains in the apartment across the way were closed. She wondered how they could have known, until she realized they must have counted the number of windows in the building to determine which apartment was hers.

It was too good to be true! She was usually shy about meeting new people, but she was just dying to introduce herself to these two women who had turned her on so much. She could hardly think straight. She stood in front of her closet for ages, going over all of her clothes. Just when she thought she had selected the perfect outfit, she would go through again and come up with something else. Finally she decided on a light, flower-print dress with a neckline that dipped low over her breasts. It was her favorite and she hoped it would be a hit with them as well.

The clock moved just as slowly as it had at work. She forced herself to sit still and eat a light dinner of cold chicken. She tried to read to pass the time, but found herself going over the same paragraph several times without comprehending any of it. When it was finally time to get ready, she enjoyed a cool shower, then tried eight different ways of arranging her hair.

At six-thirty she stood in front of the full-length mirror and assessed herself. The dress really did show off her breasts, which were full and nicely shaped. Her long legs showed the effects of frequent walks and bicycle rides; they were firm, smooth, and graceful. She gave her hair a final touch-up, dabbed on a bit of perfume, and went downstairs to wait for the taxi she had called.

When she read the address off the card to the cab driver, he took her to an area of the city she had not visited before. The street was in the heart of the city, filled with shops, restaurants, and bars.

It was a decidedly upscale area, catering to the people who worked in the tall office buildings just a few blocks away. The restaurant windows were filled with plants, and menus hung in the windows by the doors. The selection was large, and she spotted a Thai restaurant, a Japanese one, and one that specialized in Hungarian food. The bars announced their presence with neon signs, and a couple of bars boasted of brewing their own beer on the premises. Even at that early hour, the sidewalks were busy with people walking in the cooler evening air, or sitting at tables in the outdoor cafés.

The cab driver stopped at the address. It was just a door, with the number engraved on a brass plaque beside it. Wondering just what kind of place it was, Sandra paid the driver and stepped out of the cab onto the hot sidewalk.

The door was not locked, and it opened onto a flight of richly carpeted stairs leading down to a landing. Sandra could hear voices and soft music.

Downstairs she met a pleasant surprise. It was an entertainment club, and obviously private. The front part was softly lit, and she could see a well-stocked bar with stools, and several tables with comfortable chairs. There was a dance floor and a booth for a disc jockey. Toward the back, under brighter lights, were three pool tables, a shuffleboard table, and two dart boards on the wall.

There was a table beside the door, and a well-dressed woman sitting behind it. "May I help you?" she asked.

"I'm here to meet a party of two women. They're expecting me," Sandra said, and gave her name.

The woman smiled. "Of course," she said. "They're expecting you. Please go inside, they're sitting at a table by the bar."

Sandra walked in, and slowly her eyes adjusted to the low lights. To her amazement, and then delight, she noticed that there were only women inside. The bartender, the couple playing pool, the two sitting on stools at the bar were all women. Then she saw the table where the two women from the apartment were sitting.

Suddenly she found herself getting nervous this close to the women she had viewed through the window. But they smiled when they saw her, and motioned for her to come over. The seemed genuinely pleased to see her. She walked over to the table.

The tall blonde woman stood up and held out her hand. "I was sure you'd come," she said. She shook Sandra's hand. "We're glad to see you. My name is Julia, and this is Susan." The brunette woman stood up and shook hands as well.

Sandra introduced herself and at their request sat down. She noticed that they were both drinking white wine, and when the bartender came over, she ordered a glass as well.

She'd rehearsed this meeting many times in her head, but now that she was actually sitting there she felt tongue-tied. She was grateful when the wine arrived and she could fidget with the glass. "Is this a lesbian club?" she asked.

"Yes, and one of the nicest," Julia replied. "Susan and I have been members for a couple of years. It's a private club."

Sandra finally got her nerve up. "I—I hope you didn't mind me looking in your window," she said. "But I couldn't help noticing."

Susan's smile put her at ease. "We were hoping someone would," she said. "We knew it was risky, since someone might have complained. But we wanted to meet someone new. When we saw you in the window we couldn't believe how lucky we were. That's why we sent the note, and we're thrilled that you came out."

All three of them relaxed as the evening went on, and they opened up and soon were talking like old friends together. Julia and Susan offered to show Sandra the city sights, and being an excellent cook,

Sandra invited them to come to dinner at her apartment some evening. Gradually the club got a little busier, and Sandra even got an application to join.

The disc jockey came on, and a few couples made their way over to the dance floor. Julia asked Sandra to dance, and the two walked to the floor while Susan ordered another round of drinks.

Sandra felt a rush of pleasure as the tall blonde woman touched her. They moved together to a romantic song. Julia held her very close and Sandra caught her subtle, musky perfume. Her pussy was starting to feel warm as she moved with the blonde woman's motions.

"Won't Susan mind?" she whispered, glancing over to the table where the darker woman was sitting.

"Not at all," Julia replied. "In fact, she's just waiting for a chance to dance with you herself. We're very interested in you," she finished, and Sandra's heart skipped a beat. Her pussy was now on fire, and she clasped Julia's hand tightly.

Between dancing and talking, the night passed all too quickly. The three got a taxi outside the club. When the car pulled up on their street, Sandra began to give directions to her building.

Julia told the driver to let all three of them off at her own front door instead. Sandra looked at her; Julia smiled and said, "We'd like you to come upstairs for a nightcap first."

Sandra was elated with the turn of events. She rode on the elevator with the two women and waited in almost a daze while Julia unlocked the apartment door.

Everything looked so familiar. The apartment was tastefully decorated, and Sandra noticed the chair in the window where she had watched the two women begin their lovemaking. At Susan's request she sat down. The air-conditioned apartment was a welcome change from her own hot, stuffy one.

She accepted a drink. She could barely keep her eyes off the two women, who sat on the sofa facing her. Both were wearing light dresses, and their lovely bodies were shown off beautifully. Sandra longed to touch them again as she had on the dance floor.

Suddenly Julia got up and closed the curtains that had taunted Sandra all those nights. Then, before Sandra even knew what was happening, she was leaning over the chair and planting kisses on her neck.

It took Sandra a moment to realize that her fantasy was finally coming true. Her pussy burned with the knowledge, and she returned Julia's whisper-soft kisses. As she did, she could feel Susan beside her, gently stroking her throat and working her way down to the top of her dress.

"You want this, don't you?" Julia purred, and Sandra could only whisper yes. She was so excited she wanted to press her tongue right down Julia's throat. She barely knew Susan was opening the buttons on her dress until she felt the lips and tongue on her nipples. She groaned and touched Susan's full breasts through the thin dress.

"Come into the bedroom," Julia said, and the two led her to the bed she knew so well. The curtains were already closed. This performance was only going to be for the three of them.

The two undressed her as she stood before them. At Julia's insistence, she stretched out on the bed and simply enjoyed everything they were doing to her. They were as eager to give her attention as she was to receive it.

They slipped quickly out of their dresses, and Julia

admired their bodies as they bent down over hers. Susan was at her breasts, licking and sucking them and playing with her nipples. Julia was working her way down her belly to Sandra's steamy pussy, already wet with desire for the two women.

When her tongue finally reached the hard clit, Sandra almost saw stars. She moaned at the double pleasure of having both her pussy and her nipples licked at the same time. Julia was an excellent lover and she flicked over Sandra's pussy hungrily.

They kept it up fort a long time, working Sandra until she got hotter and hotter. "Do you want us?" Susan whispered huskily, and Sandra nodded. Her mouth was aching to taste them as well.

Julia stayed where she was, her tongue between Sandra's wet pussy lips. Susan got up and positioned her luscious cunt right over Sandra's waiting lips. Sandra lost no time in licking the hot clit that was above her.

It was sensational. Susan was wet and it was like licking hot syrup. Meanwhile Julia was working her pussy like crazy. Sandra had never felt anything like it before. The sounds of both of them moaning with the pleasure of their threesome turned her on even more.

Julia licked and sucked hard at Sandra's clit, and she began to tremble. Her tongue still in Susan's cunt, she groaned and shook as the hot flashes overcame her. It seemed to take forever as the orgasm exploded.

"Eat me now," Julia begged. Susan got up and the tall blonde stretched out on the bed. In an instant, Susan was crouched over her, her lover's tongue on her pussy. Sandra bent down and put her mouth to Julia's mound.

Sandra looked up as she ate Julia's sweet pussy.

Julia was busy herself in Susan's cunt, and Susan was massaging her own breasts as her pussy was being worked over.

The sight was so beautiful Sandra felt her pussy throbbing again. She reached and touched herself, rubbing her clit as she licked the blonde lips in front of her.

Susan was grinding her cunt on Julia's lips. She was very close, and Julia flicked hard at her clit until she came. At the same time, Sandra fingered herself hard and a sweet second wave rose up through her whole body. Julia was the only one left, and it didn't take long with Sandra's expert tongue in her cunt. She was very loud when she came, and Susan bent down and kissed her deeply until the last of her orgasm was over.

The three lay together on the bed, panting. "That was better than I thought it could ever be," Sandra admitted, as she ran her hand down Julia's long smooth legs.

"Fantastic!" Susan agreed, and she leaned down to kiss Sandra. Then she motioned for her to move up on the bed. Sandra wedged between them, and they calmed down from their orgasms with kisses and hugs. She felt more satisfied than she had ever been before.

Julia reached over for the light switch. Sandra started to get up, but a firm kiss from Susan held her back. "Don't leave us just yet," she begged. "You can go home in the morning."

It was just what Sandra wanted to hear, and she snuggled in between the two on the big bed. Julia whispered into her ear, "We were hoping that this wouldn't be the only time."

"It won't be," Sandra promised. They stretched out quietly for a long time, until Julia reached over and began to stroke Sandra's nipples. Happily,

Sandra reached over and put her hand between Susan's legs. Her pussy was already hot and wet, and Sandra was pleased to notice that there were still a few hours left before morning.

FOR ONE NIGHT ONLY

In Colorado, the mountains that so overwhelm visitors to the state become as natural to the residents as rain or snow. So I've been told, but even after almost eight years of living in Aspen, I still marveled at them each time I went outside. Lushly green in summer or mounded white in winter, they rose up majestically on either side of the town. Their peaks always reminded me of a woman's breasts, which could be why they held such fascination for me.

The fascination had been enough for me to arrive in Aspen for a ski trip and decide, on a moment's notice, that the flat lands back at the coast were no longer what I wanted. I moved to Aspen and eventually opened a women's clothing store in the heart of the town's shopping district. Not only did it generate enough for me to live comfortably, but it was small enough that I was able to run it myself.

Although the taller peaks were still snow-capped, the June morning was sunny and warm as I locked my front door and walked to my store. Aspen attracts tourists all year round, and I was glad to see that many of the cars parked by the sidewalk had out-of-state plates. Visitors generated most of my sales.

I stopped at the bakery near my store to pick up a coffee and muffin to take with me. "Morning, Lucy!" I called to the owner, as I poured a cup of steaming coffee.

She turned around from the oven, where she was arranging pans of bread dough. "Morning, Amy," she smiled. "You're up bright and early today."

"Figure it's the only way I can guarantee getting anything," I replied. Within the hour, Lucy's bakery would be packed with people. I had learned to get up a little earlier to beat the crowd.

It also gave me a chance to talk to Lucy, who worked long hours and didn't have a lot of time to socialize. When we discovered we were both lesbian, we naturally seemed to open up to each other, and this in turn led to a firm friendship. We had never been lovers; although we never discussed it, we both seemed to prefer a platonic relationship. It just was wonderful to have a friend who thought the same way, who shared my outlooks and concerns. On the occasional evening we got together for drinks at the bar down the street from my store.

"I just took those blueberry ones out of the oven," she said, and I picked up one of the huge muffins. It was still warm and fragrant. I put it in a bag myself, as all of Lucy's regular customers did, and left the money on the counter by the cash register.

The bread in the oven, she turned to me, wiping her floury hands on a cloth. "It's going to be pretty busy today," she said. "I've got two extra batches of bread made, and extra pies. You've got it lucky, girl. All you have to do is show people where the zipper is!"

I laughed. "I expect to be run off my feet too, today," I said. A large convention was being held in one of the resort lodges in Aspen over the next four days, and almost every hotel room in the town was booked. Aspen was a small town, with most of its stores clustered together. Tourists generally walked through all of it, stopping in each store. The merchants were quite pleased with the convention, and a lot of stores were already noticing extra sales from people who had arrived a day early.

"At least you just sell the clothes, you can't have to sew them up too!" Lucy laughed. "I've been baking since three this morning. Tell you what, though. When this crowd goes home, we'll get together and treat ourselves to a nice dinner out. What do you say?"

"You're on," I said, picking up a napkin and heading for the door. "Let me know when you're free."

It felt good to unlock the front door of my shop. It gave me great satisfaction knowing that I had done it all myself and had made a pretty good business out of it. I locked the door behind me, and went back to my little office to enjoy my coffee and muffin in peace.

By opening time everything was arranged. In the front window I had some hand-painted shirts and scarves dyed to look like Navajo blankets. Belts adorned with silver and turquoise hung near the door, with beaded moccasins below on a rack. I had long ago learned to lure tourists into the shop with clothes they couldn't buy at home, and these were my most popular items.

At nine o'clock I opened the front door and used a battered corn broom to sweep the sidewalk outside the window. Other shopkeepers up and down the street were doing the same thing, and we called good mornings to each other.

Most of the day the store enjoyed a steady stream of customers. It was obvious the convention wrapped up for the day around three, for the sidewalks were packed with people in the late afternoon and I was almost run off my feet with customers, just as I had told Lucy. As I expected, my window displays were very effective and I managed to sell a large number of the expensive hand-painted shirts and the decorated belts.

Business died down around six, and now it was time for me to take a breather while the restaurants scurried to keep up with the crowds. My store was empty for the first time and I took advantage of it to unwrap the sandwich I had bought earlier in the day.

I only got a couple of bites when a woman walked in. I could only stare. She was gorgeous. She had a model's face, or a movie star's, with fine features and enormous brown eyes. Her hair was carefully arranged and she was expensively dressed. I wanted her as soon as I laid eyes on her. She was so sensuous, so graceful.

My sandwich was forgotten. "Are you looking for anything specific?" I asked, as she looked over a rack of shirts by the window.

She turned to me. Was I imagining it, or did I catch a spark in her eyes? "I'm looking for a dress," she said. "A summery one, something light."

I led her to the back of the store where the dresses were. I could smell her perfume and I wanted to touch her hair. My pussy was stirring as I looked her over, trying to decide on which style I should show her.

"How about this?" I asked. I pulled out a rich red dress that would show off her breasts. "Or maybe something shorter?" I found a lovely purple one.

"Let me try the red one," she said, smiling at me. I showed her where the fitting room was. She disappeared inside. I wished I could have gone with her to help her undress.

She came out shortly in the bright red dress. As I expected, it hung perfectly on her. It was low in front and the tops of her creamy breasts were so inviting.

"That is gorgeous!" I said, as she moved in front of the full-length mirror. It really did suit her, and she knew it. She caught my eyes in the mirror and again smiled at me.

She turned around to face me, and tugged at the neckline. "Do you think this sits right?" she asked. "Is this how it's supposed to fit?"

I reached for the fabric. "That's the way—" I stopped. She had leaned into me, so that my hand pressed against her warm breast. "Oh—excuse me," I said.

"No need to," she smiled. She looked again in the mirror. "You're right, it's perfect. I'll take it."

She went back into the changing room. I didn't know what to think. She had obviously gone out of her way to set me up and push against me. I could still feel her body against my hand, and the sensation made my pussy tingle. I didn't dare believe that she wanted me, but I wished with all my heart that she did.

She came out, and I took the dress to the counter and began to wrap it in tissue paper.

"Are you here for the convention?" I asked.

"Only for today," she said. "I had to give a seminar, but I have to be back in New York tomorrow morning. It's a shame, really. This is a beautiful place and I wish I could stay longer and see it."

I slipped the dress inside a bag. She handed over her credit card. Sharon MacMillan. I wanted to speak her name, to whisper in her ear.

"So," she said, "what do people do in this town for excitement on a Thursday night?"

"Well, there's a lot of good restaurants, and there's live entertainment in the lounge down the street," I said.

She glanced around to be sure the store was empty, then leaned toward me. "Maybe you'd like to show me around. After all, I'm only here for one night."

My heart was beating so hard I thought she could hear it. Although I wanted her, I suddenly found myself as flustered as a schoolgirl at her boldness. "I don't close the shop until nine o'clock," I stammered.

She was cool as could be, and I envied her and wanted her both at the same time. "Then I'll be back at nine," she said. "You look like the type who could show a lady a good time—are you?"

"Yes," I said, almost in a whisper. Then to my surprise, she picked up the bag, leaned over the counter and kissed me on the lips. I was shocked at first, but in seconds I was returning it. Her lips were warm and smooth, and her tongue darted out to tease mine ever so gently. Then she stood up straight.

"Nine o'clock," she promised, and left the store.

I went limp with desire. This was the sort of thing I read in magazines! But here it was, happening to me, right in my own store. My pussy was throbbing so badly I couldn't stand it. I rushed and locked the door.

I hurried into the changing room. I just couldn't bear the unsatisfied heat any longer. I pulled up my skirt and slipped off my panties. Sitting in the chair, facing the mirror, I saw my wet pussy. My hand was on my clit in seconds. Each flick of my finger was Sharon's tongue massaging my hot cunt lips. I slipped a finger inside my wet hole, and imagined that it was her finger feeling me up. My tongue darted in my mouth. I wanted to lick her pussy so badly I could almost taste it.

I watched myself in the mirror as I rubbed my pussy. My fingers were wet with my hot juice and they looked so good against the dark hair. My hand went up to hold my breast and twist the nipple through my shirt. I could feel her hands on them. I wanted to feel her hands on my cunt.

Normally I teased myself and took a long time when I made myself come. Now I was so horny I couldn't wait. My clit was so hard and rubbing it felt so good. My nipples were erect and I could see them through my shirt. I pulled them hard, gasping at how delicious it felt.

I rubbed harder and faster. I worked myself up to an edge, then let myself fall over it into my orgasm. It was wonderful. I fingered myself until the last of it was finished. I sat for a few moments to collect myself, then I straightened my dress and went back to open the store.

I went through the rest of the day almost in a dream. I had never been approached in such a way before. Sharon's shameless advances had turned me on. And that saucy kiss! No one had ever done that before. This was a very strong woman, one who would control me, and the idea was exciting. I longed to melt in her arms and let her do with me whatever she wanted.

At eight thirty I decided to close up early, the first time I had ever done so. I then went back into the shop and went through the racks of dresses. I found one that had just come in the week before, a beautiful pale silk one. I tried it on. It fit perfectly and I thought it was stunning. I hung up my own dress in the back room, fixed my hair, and decided I would worry about accounting for the dress in the stock books tomorrow.

At nine o'clock I heard a tapping at the glass door. Sharon was right on time. She was dressed in a softly tailored suit that showed off her beautiful body to full advantage. I opened the door and she walked into the store.

"You look lovely," she said. "Are you closed for the night? Good, let's go get something to eat. I'm starving."

I suggested a restaurant on the next block, and she agreed. The night was pleasantly warm and we walked over.

The restaurant was dark and quiet. We were led to a table by the window, where we could watch people walking by and see the mountains that rose up at the edge of town.

We both ordered cocktails, and the server brought us a menu. When it arrived, Sharon lifted her glass in a toast. "I'm glad I met you today," she said. "I'm usually lost in the evenings when I have to go on business trips. This is so pleasant."

"It's a nice change for me, too," I admitted. "I usually just go home and stick some dinner in the microwave, then go to bed with a book. It's nice to have my own store, but it sure means long hours."

We ordered dinner, and Sharon asked for a bottle of wine. She sat back and looked out the window. "I've never been in Colorado before," she said. "This is a beautiful place. I can understand why you live here."

"Where are you staying?" I asked.

"At a lodge just outside of town," she said. "Have you ever been inside it?" I admitted I hadn't.

She reached over and put her hand on mine. Her soft touch sent ripples through me. "Then you must come back with me and see it," she said. "I'm only here for tonight. You may not get the chance again."

My pussy was burning. I hardly even noticed what my appetizer was. All I saw were Sharon's rich, full lips and her soft hands. I wanted them on my body, and it looked as if I was going to get my wish.

She definitely wasn't subtle. Putting down her fork, she leaned across the table and looked deep into my eyes. "I want you," she said.

"I was hoping you would," I whispered. "I think you're beautiful."

She smiled. "Then let's enjoy our dinner," she said. "Fine dining is a sensual experience too. Then we can go back to my room for dessert."

She was definitely a connoisseur. The wine she had ordered matched perfectly with our food, which the restaurant had prepared in its usual impeccable style. Sharon was impressed with the quality, and admitted that it rivaled some of the finer restaurants she frequented in New York. It filled me with pride to hear her say that.

Our evening decided, Sharon switched the conversation easily. She asked about the store and my lifestyle in Aspen, and seemed genuinely interested in my answers. She told me she was a consultant for a large New York computer firm, which not only accounted for her hectic business trips but also for the fact that she refused to let me pay anything for the expensive dinner.

I enjoyed her company immensely. The time flew by, and before I knew it, it was eleven o'clock. When our coffee was finished, she asked if I was still interested in seeing her room. What a question! My pussy had been on fire throughout the entire dinner.

We walked back to my store. Sharon's car, a rented Cadillac sedan, was parked in front. It was quite a switch from my little Chevy, and I stretched out on the comfortable seat.

Within minutes we were outside of Aspen. The lodge was a beautiful one, tucked up at the base of the mountain for skiing in winter. At the front door, the valet held the car doors open for us, then got in himself and drove it away.

The front lobby was beautifully decorated, but that wasn't what I wanted to see. We went up on the elevator, and I waited while Sharon opened the door to her room.

Sharon must have been as hot as I was. As soon as she closed the door behind us, I found myself in her arms, her mouth on mine. It felt so good to let myself go. I returned her kiss. She pressed her tongue inside my mouth, and my own rose to meet it. My pussy was already wet as she ran her hands down my neck and held my breasts through my dress.

I reached for hers. They were firm and felt heavy in my hands. She kissed me for what seemed like hours. Her mouth was sweet and her kisses were like honey. Her tongue moved so beautifully in my mouth I thought that she might be able to make me come just like that.

Finally she stepped back and began to unbutton my dress. I reached for her, but she gently pushed my hands down. "Let me," she said. "You just relax. I want to make love to you."

She pushed the dress off my shoulders and it fell

to the floor. "You are exquisite," she said, and bent down to nibble at my breasts through my bra. Once again she would not let me raise my hands. I could only stand there and enjoy everything she was doing to me.

She kissed me deeply as she reached around my back to unhook my bra. She murmured approval, and immediately bent down and licked my nipple. I moaned. Her mouth was just as I had imagined it would be. My pussy was now throbbing hard and I longed for relief.

She turned me around and lowered me onto the bed. "I love your tits!" she whispered and showed her appreciation. I had never had such attention lavished on them. She ran her hands under them and pushed them together, then sucked my nipples into her mouth and licked the tips of them. She rubbed her own nipples over them, through her clothes. She tickled them with her hair, and blew gently on them to cool them off. Then she took them into her warm mouth. That made me groan with pleasure.

"Please let me see you," I begged. She sucked my nipples for a little while longer, then stood up. She took her clothes off slowly. Her body was magnificent. She really did look like a model with her firm breasts and slim waist. Her pussy was dark and I wanted more than anything to put my tongue in between her hairy lips. She even surprised me with a tiny butterfly tattoo on her hip.

She then returned to me. It turned her on to give me pleasure and she did a beautiful job. She made me roll over, and she ran her fingernails up and down my back for a long time. Then she used her tongue, moving slowly down my body until she reached my ass. Here she used her tongue to tease me, flicking it between my cheeks while she kneaded my ass with her fingers. I could only lie on the bed and soak up her attention. It was wonderful beyond comprehension.

"Roll over," she said, and I was only too happy to. Again she used her tongue to draw long strokes on my body, from my breasts down to my belly. I was getting hotter and hotter as she moved closer to my soaked pussy.

My hands moved up to touch her, but each time she gently put them back at my sides. "Just enjoy it," she said. "You'll get your turn later."

It was easy to enjoy what she was doing. She licked down to my hair, then went right around my throbbing pussy and licked the insides of my thighs. It was heavenly. Her touch was so soft as she thrilled me with her mouth.

Her first flick across my clit made me gasp. She licked me slowly the whole length of my pussy. I shivered and moaned as she stroked my clit with just the tip of her tongue.

She licked her finger, then slowly pushed it into my hole. The lubrication wasn't necessary. I was so wet I could feel my hot juice on the insides of my thighs. She slowly fucked me with one finger, then two. It was a wonderful full feeling, and even better when she went back to licking my clit as she pushed her fingers inside.

"Tell me how good it feels," she said. "I like to hear what you're feeling." She pushed her tongue under the folds of my pussy lips and ran it around the top of my cunt.

"It feels so good!" I gasped. "Your tongue—right there! Oh yes, lick me on that spot!"

"Tell me about it," she said. She slipped her hand down to tickle at my ass. I couldn't stop my hips from moving.

"It feels so warm," I said. It really did, both the

warmth from her wet tongue and the heat that was constantly building up inside me. "It's so warm, and it's just like all of you is inside me!"

She teased me. She would suck hard at my clit for a while until I got close to coming, then back off and lap slowly. The buildup was beautiful.

"Would you like to come now?" she asked. I was so worked up I could only nod, and I felt her tongue move up my pussy to my clit.

Her tongue moved so fast I couldn't believe it. I got closer and closer and then without warning the cascade started in my cunt and flooded over me. Still I wanted more, and she didn't stop. Within a few seconds, a second wave filled me and I cried out. It was so intense! My whole body was on fire as she licked the last few shivers out of me.

She stretched out beside me, idly drawing circles around my nipple with her fingernail. "It was nice, wasn't it?" she purred. I could only whisper a yes; I was still coming down from my explosive orgasm. "I knew it would be." She bent down and kissed my lips.

In one swift move she was over me, straddling my face with her beautiful pussy. I had waited so long for this. I could smell her lovely aroma and see the glistening lips. "Bring it down to me," I begged. "Let me lick your pussy!"

She did. Her cunt was rich and sweet. I held her ass cheeks and kneaded them while my tongue danced over her clit. I pulled her down so that my tongue fitted into her hole, and fucked her with it. My whole face was wet with her honey.

She moaned as I flitted over her pussy. I tried to be as slow and teasing as she had been with me, but it was impossible. She was going wild on my tongue. She moved her hips and ground her sweet pussy on my mouth. I ate her furiously. I loved having her cunt right on my face and her clit in my mouth.

"Lick me harder!" she begged. I concentrated all of my efforts on the hard nub of flesh. She began to moan, then gasped and cried out as she came. I was buried in her pussy. She trembled for a long time and I licked slowly at her until she finally got up and lay down beside me.

"Wonderful," she gasped, and kissed me again. "That was just fantastic." I ran my hands up and down her firm body and hugged her tightly.

We held each other for a long time. She reached up and smoothed my hair back from my face and gently kissed my cheek and eyelids. "I'm so glad I ran into you today," she said. "I haven't had anything that nice for so long."

"I haven't either," I said. "No one's ever eaten me like that before."

She kissed me again. "I have to be up at five to catch my plane," she said. "I can take you back to your house and you'll have lots of time to open your store. Will you please stay the night with me?"

Would I! I felt so satisfied and content, I couldn't imagine getting up and leaving. "Of course," I said. Sharon motioned for me to move so that she could pull the covers up over ourselves. I snuggled into her arms and we spent another hour just talking.

"I wish I didn't have to go so soon," she said. "I'd really like to get to know you better."

"I'm always here," I said. "You know where my store is. I'm sure you'll be back for another meeting sometime."

She smiled. "If not, then I guess I could always learn to ski. It would be a perfect excuse for a trip."

Finally she turned the light out. I fell into such a deep sleep it seemed like only minutes before the wake-up call disturbed us. Sharon kissed me and we dressed and went downstairs to where the car was waiting at the front door.

She drove me into town and stopped in front of my house. The street was still empty at that early hour.

She leaned over and kissed me, a long, gentle kiss. "I only wish we could have had more time," she said.

"So do I," I said. "It really was wonderful."

She reached into her pocket and pulled out a business card. "I'm definitely going to try to get back here soon," she said. "In the meantime, if you come out New York way, please let me know." I promised I would.

Reluctantly I got out of the car and closed the door. There was one last look, and then she pulled away from the curb. I watched the car until she finally turned the corner out of sight.

Back to my regular routine. I went in the house, showered and dressed, and watered the plants. Then I grabbed my bag and began my familiar route to work.

Lucy was making rolls in the empty bakery. I let the wooden screen door slam, as I always did, and called out my good morning as I reached for a cup and the pot of coffee.

"Morning, Amy!" she called out. "So what's new with you?"

I put the coffee pot back on the burner, then leaned over the counter and took a sip. "Lucy," I began, "you wouldn't believe it."

NAUGHTY GIRL

It's hard for me to pinpoint exactly the moment that I knew I enjoyed being spanked. Judy had always been an aggressive lover and I was satisfied to put myself under her control. I submitted to her whims, and was always ready when she told me to get undressed or to lick her waiting pussy. We gradually discovered that spanking was an important part of sex for us, and that it excited us both. Just the thought of her hand smacking my bare ass was enough to set my pussy on fire.

It had begun with friendly pats on my ass, and light slaps when we were making love. I soon realized that these gentle smacks were turning good sex into great sex, and I begged her to apply her hand a little harder. It thrilled me when she did so eagerly. Soon she was spanking me hard, and I was loving every minute of it. When I couldn't sit down afterward, I loved it most of all.

One day she admitted that turning me over her knee and whacking my behind was just as exciting for her as it was for me. I couldn't have been happier. Since that day, we regularly sent each other into ecstasy with sex and spankings.

Judy never gave me much warning before a spanking, which made it even more exciting for me. I never knew when her hand would strike and give me the delicious punishment I longed for. Sometimes I went through the house setting little traps in the hope that she would decide I needed to be spanked. Sometimes it was letting the garbage can overfill, or not putting the cap back on the shampoo bottle. Leaving the milk carton on the counter, instead of putting it back in the refrigerator, was almost always guaranteed to set her off.

"Angela!" I heard her shout as I sat in the living room reading a book. "Angela, come here immediately!"

I knew better than to disobey Judy when she used that voice. I walked slowly into the kitchen. Already my pussy was stirring and I felt giddy with desire. I knew what I was in for.

She pointed to the counter where the offending carton stood. "After last time, I didn't think I'd have to remind you again!" she said. "What do you have to say for yourself?"

I hung my head. "I forgot," I mumbled. "I was in a hurry." I was getting so horny I could hardly stand up.

Instantly I felt Judy's strong hand on the back of my neck. "That's just not good enough," she said, steering me toward our bedroom. "I think you need another lesson so you won't forget next time."

Within seconds my shorts were down around my

ankles, followed quickly by my panties. Judy sat on the bed and pulled me across her knees. I held my breath and waited.

The first crack of her hand across my buttocks made me gasp. It stung, and tears popped into my eyes. My pussy was throbbing now.

Slap! Another crack from her firm hand. "Please!" I cried out. "I'll be good! I won't ever forget again!"

"That's why you need this," she answered firmly. "To make sure you don't forget again."

Another smack, and another. I could picture my ass cheeks, stinging and red, with the imprint of her hand on them. My face was burning and I knew it must be as bright red as my behind. The pain in my ass and the heat in my pussy were almost too much to stand.

I was crying now, as Judy continued my punishment. Then she reached under me and her finger rubbed against my clit, as her other hand continued to fall on my tender ass cheeks.

She calmly counted out the blows. Four! Her finger pushed against my hard clit and I gasped. Five! I squirmed and ground my pussy on her hand. I could feel how wet her fingers were with my juice. Six! Her thumb played with my hole.

The whipping went on. Sometimes she hit one buttock and then the other, sometimes her hand landed across both. I was crying now, and I could feel the pressure building in my pussy as her fingers moved in my cunt.

I didn't get my usual ten. As she counted to nine and her hand spanked my ass, she rubbed hard on my clit. Groaning with both the pleasure and the pain, I exploded in a beautiful orgasm.

Judy was suddenly as gentle as could be, running her hand soothingly over my bruised behind. My skin was stinging. It felt as good as my pussy did.

The spanking had turned Judy on just as much. "I think you've learned your lesson this time," she said. "Now I want you to thank me for your discipline."

I needed no encouragement. I took off my shirt while she undressed and lay on her back. I parted her legs. I could see that her beautiful pussy was already glistening with her honey.

She was delicious. She moaned as I put my tongue deep in her hole and then licked all around it. Her clit was hard and hot and I moved it back and forth with my lips. Her hands were on my head, pushing my mouth hard against her sweet, sexy pussy.

The rich taste of her juice filled my mouth like wine. My ass still burned from my spanking and it spurred me on. I licked her hard, my tongue flicking fast over her clit. She was loving her tongue-lashing, squirming and grinding herself into me.

She was so worked up it didn't take long for her to come. She cried out as she did, her hips bucking crazily and her clit rubbing hard on my tongue. The heady smell of sex hung over us in the air like musky perfume. We collapsed together on the bed, both of us totally satisfied.

"I hope this teaches you not to cross me again," she said, as I ran my hand over her body.

"Oh, yes," I said, but both of us knew that it wouldn't be long before I would find a way to earn another lesson—providing that Judy didn't find a reason first.

As it turned out, it was only a few days before Judy once again found it necessary to discipline me. Of course I took the logical course and blamed the postman. Just when it became comfortable to sit down again, too!

I got home from work before Judy did, and when I emptied the mailbox I found a parcel addressed to her. Curiosity had always been one of my downfalls, and it was working overtime on that particular day. I didn't recognize the return address, a box number in San Francisco. There was nothing printed on the box to give any clue as to its contents.

It wasn't overly heavy. I shook it, but there was only a dull rustling inside, like something wrapped in crumpled paper shifting about. I tried to peek under the flap of the box, but it was securely glued shut.

I was so busy trying to guess what was in the box I didn't hear Judy come into the house. I didn't even realize she was standing beside me until the package was roughly pulled out of my hands.

Her voice was calm but icy, and it sent a luscious chill down my spine. I knew right away I was in pretty deep trouble. "You should know better than to pry into my private mail," she said. "I guess you've forgotten everything you learned. You're going to need another lesson."

I wanted her so badly I was almost dizzy. "Do you want me to take off my pants?" I asked. I could almost feel her hand connecting with my ass. I wanted to be hauled over her knees, with my tender backside ready for her.

"Oh, no," she replied, giving me a look that was both firm and seductive at the same time. "Only animals have to be punished as soon as they're caught doing something wrong."

She reached down and gently stroked my cheek with the tips of her fingers. Her touch was so distant and cold, her fingers felt icy and bloodless, and I shivered. "I'm withholding your punishment until I feel it's the right time. That way, you can think about what you've done, and why you must be disciplined. Maybe then the lesson will sink in better."

She knew how to get to me! My pussy would probably drive me crazy waiting for my spanking. I thought it was the ultimate in discipline until she revealed another trick that I knew would leave me climbing the walls.

Slowly she opened the forbidden box that had been the source of all my woes. As I had suspected, it was filled with crumpled newspaper. Inside was an object wrapped in a heavy plastic bag.

She broke the bag open, and slowly pulled the object out. I gasped, and went almost shaky with desire.

It was a leather paddle, with a heavy wooden grip. Without flinching, she slapped her palm with it twice. The crack of the leather against her skin was like a gunshot. I shivered.

She put it down on the table and put the newspaper back in the box. "You may look at it if you like," she said, picking up the box and walking into the kitchen. "Just remember that your little transgression will not be forgotten. Sooner or later I will put that to good use."

I always knew Judy was very good at disciplining me, but as I stared at the paddle, fascinated, I realized I was in the hands of an expert. My day at work, my plans for dinner, everything was forgotten as I looked it over. My mind was concentrated on only one thing. Already I could feel a tingling on my ass cheeks, and a stir in my pussy.

How long before I would feel that black leather against my ass? I picked it up. It was heavy, with a good, solid wood handle. The leather was thick and smelled delicious. I bent the edge. It was somewhat supple, but still firm. It wouldn't deliver wimpy little taps. This device was made to see active duty.

I slapped my palm with it gently. It made a lot of noise, and it managed to deliver a pleasant sting. I slapped my hand harder. This time it really hurt, and my hand immediately turned red. There was no getting away from it: I was really going to feel the effects of my curiosity!

I must have played with it longer than I thought, for soon Judy was calling me to the dining room for supper. I put the paddle back on the coffee table and hurried in, lest she use my dawdling as another reason for a spanking.

She was pouring wine into crystal glasses. "You are so forgetful, Angela," she said. "Bring that paddle in with you."

I hurried back to get it. I sat down at my place, and Judy positioned the paddle on the far corner of the table. My eyes never left it. I ate my dinner, but hardly noticed what I was putting in my mouth. Even the expensive wine had no taste for me that night. Every fiber of my being was concentrated on that beautiful leather paddle. My pussy was throbbing so badly I had to squirm on my chair for relief.

Judy noticed all of it. "It does look quite effective, doesn't it?" she asked. "I'll bet your little ass is going to be as red as a cherry when I'm through with you."

I suffered through dessert and coffee, my eyes on the leather paddle. I was sure Judy was taking longer than usual to eat, and she sat at the table for the longest time before bringing out the dessert. She even had a third cup of coffee, which she had never done before. She was playing this out as long as she possibly could.

I didn't even get a break when I washed the dishes, for Judy made sure that the paddle sat on the corner of the kitchen counter while I worked. I left a tiny crumb of food on one of the plates by mistake, and Judy coldly promised that I would receive an extra smack for that.

I followed her as she carried the paddle into the living room. It sat on the table as she relaxed on the sofa and read a book. Occasionally she would reach over and touch it. My own book was still on the table, unopened; I couldn't think about anything else. I was amazed at how excited I was.

Finally she placed her bookmark carefully and set the book down. "Take off your clothes," she ordered.

My legs were like jelly and it was difficult to stand up and undress. Somehow I managed. Judy then took off her own clothes. I loved the sight of her beautiful body. Her nipples were so large and firm, and her luscious pussy was surrounded by thick, dark hair.

She sat on the edge of the sofa, her legs apart. "Come here," she said. "On your hands and knees."

I did. The rough carpet bit into my skin. I could feel how wet my pussy was, and also how vulnerable my ass cheeks were. In that position, I was completely at her mercy. I both dreaded and longed for that paddle.

Judy reached out and pulled my head toward her pussy. "Eat me!" she ordered.

Her pussy was already wet, and I realized she must have worked herself up over my punishment as well. I didn't need to be ordered to lick her beautiful cunt. I loved doing it. I circled her tight hole with my tongue, then pushed her clit back and forth with just the tip.

CRACK! I almost screamed. It hurt like hell, and the wide paddle covered all of my ass in a single stroke. I could picture my buttocks going bone-white right after the stroke, then flushing bright red. I went dizzy, and for a moment I thought I might faint. Then the stinging set in.

The exquisite pain flowed right to my pussy, and I moaned with desire. Through a fog I heard Judy tell me to keep on licking her.

"Please be gentle," I whispered, and put my tongue back in her cunt. I was crazy for her. My tongue whipped over her clit and lapped up her sweet juice. My own pussy was begging for the same kind of attention.

Crack! My eyes welled up with tears. This time I didn't stop licking her, and she groaned with pleasure and approval.

The paddle smashed down again and again. I was crying openly, and as the tears ran down my face, I tasted their salty warmth mingled with the sweet, rich taste of Judy's cunt.

My own pussy was throbbing so badly I finally reached back and touched my clit with my fingers. "That's it!" Judy gasped. "Make us both come!" I licked hard at her delicious pussy while I fingered myself.

Four more times the wicked leather paddle smashed down on my burning ass. My tears were streaming but I didn't stop licking Judy or fingering my own pussy for a moment. It all felt so good.

"Lick me hard!" Judy gasped, and cracked the paddle down again. I sucked as hard as I could on her clit. She began to tremble, then cried out as she came.

I was so close myself. The leather slapped my ass again and I rubbed my clit hard. It was fantastic! The combination of pleasure and pain filled my pussy and I almost screamed as I came.

I struggled to catch my breath. "Come up here," Judy said, and made me lie down on my stomach. My poor ass felt raw and blistered. The paddle certainly was effective.

Judy left the room and came back with a bottle of lotion. Gently she rubbed it into my ass cheeks. "Your skin is so red, you poor thing," she said. "Let me make it better."

The lotion felt cool and soothing on my hot skin. I

wiped my tears away and enjoyed the soft touch of her hand. She rubbed me a long time, eventually giving me a complete back rub with the scented lotion. It felt so relaxing I finally fell asleep right there on the sofa. When I woke up an hour later, my ass felt swollen and tight and I had to spend the rest of the evening either standing up or lying on my stomach. Every now and again I would reach behind and gently pat my ass. The stinging reminded me of the flogging I had received, and the memory gave me sweet little twinges in my pussy.

Fortunately I didn't have to sit down at work much the next day. Each time I did, I received a quick and painful reminder of my lesson. Judy had informed me that she expected no further problems from me, but as usual, we both knew otherwise. She had hidden the paddle somewhere in the house and I was just waiting for my bruised ass to heal so that I could get into more trouble!

Judy spent the next week just teasing me. One afternoon I went into the house and found the leather paddle on the table in the hallway. I picked it up and gently stroked my cheek with it. I sniffed deeply, enjoying the musky animal smell of the leather. I almost imagined I could smell my own scent on it, my hot pussy and my blistered cheeks. I kissed it. I put it back carefully, but an hour after Judy came home, it had disappeared.

It turned up again on my dresser, and on top of the refrigerator. Just the sight of it made me weak with desire. I loved to catch the first glimpse of it out of the corner of my eye, and I was always looking for it. Judy never mentioned it and when she walked in once as I was picking it up, she ignored me and walked out again. Each time it would be gone after a couple of hours, and I did not know where she was hiding it.

Finally I could take her teasing no longer. It wasn't enough just to catch sight of that nasty black paddle; I wanted to feel it on me. Once again I tried to figure out something that Judy would feel deserved a whipping.

I left my towel in a heap on the bathroom floor and a pair of socks on the sofa, but Judy was just as determined to continue with her teasing. I found the towel neatly hung up, with the paddle on the bathroom sink. My socks were left in a pile on the sofa, with the paddle beside them. Each time, it would be whisked away an hour or two later. I could barely think straight, my pussy was so tight and tingly. I wanted that paddle so badly I was considering just taking it to her and demanding that she use it on my behind.

I finally hit paydirt with the newspaper. Judy always read it cover to cover each evening, and it was always wedged in the door by the paperboy when I came home from work. Unfailingly, I left it undisturbed on the coffee table for her, for Judy was very adamant about the condition of her newspaper. She had to be the first one to open it, and she disliked anyone rifling through it before she got a chance to. Finding it opened or the sections out of order would easily put her in a very foul mood.

I was just too hot for a lick of that paddle across my ass. I opened the paper and scattered the sections around the living room. I even took a couple of pages out of the news section and draped them over the dining room chairs. Then I changed into a light summer dress, with no underwear beneath it, and waited for Judy to come home and witness the dismantling of the evening news.

She was smiling when she walked through the door, but it quickly turned to a bitter frown when she walked into the living room and saw her paper scattered all over. Her eyes grew as cold as gray glass and her cheeks colored. I knew I was finally going to get my wish.

"Angela," she said, "what's the meaning of this?"

"I don't know," I replied, in a little-girl voice. "I didn't do it. I came home and this is what I found. It was just all over like this, honest."

She turned to me. Her eyes were still cold but I could detect a hot spark that I knew was rapidly growing. "This is terrible," she said. "First you destroy my paper, and then you lie to me about it. What are we going to do about this?"

I looked down at the floor. "Please be gentle," I said. "Please don't hurt me. I won't do it again, I promise."

"I think you need a lesson about leaving the newspaper alone, don't you?" she continued.

"I won't do it again," I repeated in a whimper.

"That's not good enough," Judy said. She walked across the room and reached inside the cabinet where we kept our videotapes. So that's where it had been hidden!

The sight of the black paddle in her hand was delicious. I could feel my pussy getting hot and wet. She slapped it against her palm, and the sharp crack made me jump.

"Now, you naughty girl," she said, "take off your dress."

I did. My nipples were hard as rocks and stood out urgently. My pussy was burning between my legs. I watched as Judy took off her dress as well. She looked so sexy, her beautiful tits and her dark pussy, and the cruel leather device in her hand. I wanted her so badly I didn't know how long I could wait.

She led me over to the sofa and made me kneel on

it. Then she pushed me down so that I was bent over the thickly padded arm. My ass was sticking up in the air, a perfect target for her leather friend. She pushed my legs apart so that my wet pussy was accessible.

She got on the sofa behind me. With my head down I couldn't see what she was doing. I tensed my bottom, expecting the firm crash of leather on my cheeks at any moment.

To my surprise, instead of the hard leather, I felt Judy's soft, warm tongue in my pussy. I groaned as she licked my hole and sucked my clit. I was confused. It felt so good and her touch was so tender, so different from the punishment I was expecting. Then just as suddenly it stopped.

Wham! The paddle came down with a sharp crack on my ass. The familiar searing pain shot through me. I cried out.

Again the paddle struck. Judy was right over me and was able to hit me with all her strength. It knocked the breath out of me and I tasted my tears. I was not going to forget this lesson quickly.

Then she leaned back and once again I felt her soft, feathery tongue on my steamy pussy. I was so confused by the blistering leather and her sweet tongue that I didn't know which felt better.

"Your ass is so red," Judy whispered, "and your pussy is so good and wet!" She licked slowly at my clit, and reached up to tease my asshole with her tongue. Gently she spread my ass cheeks apart, but I almost screamed when I felt her hands on me. My behind was so tender it hurt for her to touch me.

Her tongue on my clit was bringing me close to orgasm, but I knew she wouldn't let me go so quickly. Just as my body began to tense up, she stopped licking me and leaned back.

This time she didn't use the paddle. Instead, I felt

her firm hand spanking me hard. It didn't make as much noise as the leather, but it hurt me almost as much. She slapped both cheeks hard, then began a steady rhythm, counting out each blow as it landed on my sore skin.

"One!" she said. Her hand smacked against my ass and I cried out. "Don't use up all your tears yet," she warned. "You've been very naughty and I'm not finished with you!"

Two! This one landed across both cheeks with a resounding crack. I whimpered. My clit felt so hard and swollen I thought it might burst.

Three! Four! Five! I knew my ass was flaming red, and the skin was burning. Six! Seven! I was almost beside myself, and I wanted her tongue back on my pussy desperately.

She obliged me after two more hard smacks. My pussy felt creamy as her tongue glided back and forth over it. I could feel my juice on my thighs. It was as hot as the burning skin on my ass.

"Your cunt tastes so good," she purred, and stuck her tongue deep in my hole. I moaned with pleasure. She stuck two fingers in my wet hole and fucked me with them, rubbing my clit at the same time with her thumb.

I squirmed and pushed my clit against her. Her voice was soft and soothing. "That feels good, doesn't it?" she cooed. "Your pussy is so wet and so warm, my fingers are just sliding in. Oh, that must feel so nice."

Crack! I cried out as the leather paddle bit into my behind. Judy never stopped moving her fingers on my cunt. The pain and pleasure mingled together and I sobbed loudly. I couldn't see for the tears in my eyes.

Smack! The paddle landed again, and again. The

pain felt like boiling liquid flowing through the muscles of my ass. Then Judy bent down and sucked hard on my swollen clit.

It was too much. My climax was shattering. She kept licking me, and I just kept coming. I was dizzy as I cried out, bent over the sofa arm, my ass burning white-hot from my spanking, my clit sizzling from my licking.

Judy was just as excited. "Suck me now!" she ordered, and I turned around. She was already on her back, her legs spread apart and her pussy waiting for me.

I didn't need to be told twice. Within seconds I was down between her legs, inhaling the gorgeous thick scent of her sex. I thought her pussy would burn my tongue. She was wet all over and my tongue slid over her smooth, buttery flesh.

Her hands were on her breasts while I ate her, her fingers pulling and twisting her nipples. I loved the sight of her doing that, and it made me lick her faster and faster. She was moaning loudly and every so often she reached down and pushed my mouth hard against her clit. I took it between my lips and sucked on it, and she lifted her hips to grind it against me.

"Lick me! Lick me harder!" she cried. We were both in a frenzy, both of us soaked with sweat and very excited by my spanking. My tongue just couldn't go any faster on her.

I plunged my tongue again and again onto her clit, flicking it from side to side. Judy tensed up and shouted, "Lick me! Lick me! Ooh!" Then she came, with my tongue still firmly against her juicy clit. I loved every minute of it.

She hugged me tightly for a moment, then got up and retrieved the bottle of lotion. Once again I stretched out on the sofa and was treated to a delicious soothing massage on my fiery buttocks. I had never been spanked that hard before.

The paddle, damp with sweat, lay on the coffee table, as menacing as ever. I almost worshiped it. I shivered, and closed my eyes to enjoy Judy's light touch. She was so gentle I could hardly believe it was the same woman who had so firmly tanned my hide earlier.

"So, you naughty girl," she asked, while pouring on more cool lotion, "did you learn your lesson this time?"

"Oh, yes," I said quickly. I reached up to wipe away the last of my tears, and I knew my eyes were red and swollen also.

She continued to rub the lotion into my skin, pausing every now and again to plant a kiss on my stinging cheeks. She also stopped frequently for a kiss on my lips, and our warm tongues mingled with love and the memory of the fantastic sex we'd just shared.

I glanced over at the paddle. Even though my ass was burning, I was looking forward to another session of being at the paddle's mercy. Perhaps I had learned my lesson about the newspaper, but I knew for sure I'd soon be looking for new reasons for Judy to take me over her knee and give me a good old-fashioned spanking.

BEAUTIFUL BONDS

"She's at the booth in the corner, if you're interested."

Anne took the drink offered to her by the bartender, then looked around the room. It was difficult, for the lesbian bar was very popular, and was always filled and very smoky on Friday nights. She finally caught sight of the woman in the booth, who was watching her very intently from across the room.

Anne couldn't see her completely, but she noticed the heavy black leather motorcycle jacket right away. It definitely piqued her interest, and she felt the quick tingles in her pussy that she always had when she thought about women in leather. It was promising. Perhaps this would be the woman who would give her what she really wanted this night. It had been so long, and she was so damn horny. She picked up the drink—a perfectly mixed Manhattan, her usual order—and made her way through the crowded room.

She stood beside the booth, until the leather-clad woman motioned for her to sit down. She slipped into the empty seat opposite her. "Thank you for the drink," she said. "My name's Anne."

"My pleasure, Anne," the woman replied. "My name's Catherine. I saw you sitting up there and you looked pretty lonely, so I figured you might like some company."

Anne looked her over and was excited by what she saw. Catherine was a tall woman, with heavy breasts. Anne could tell because she wore nothing under the motorcycle jacket.

She was dressed entirely in leather. The sight made Anne catch her breath. The tight pants she wore were black leather like her jacket, and on her feet she wore heavy motorcycle boots with silver chains wrapped around the ankles and leather straps running under the soles. Catherine shifted, and Anne heard the noise they made. She peeked under the table. The sight sent a shiver down her spine. She absolutely loved the sight of chains, especially when they were wrapped firmly around something and locked tight.

Catherine noticed her right away, and she smiled. "You like those chains, do you?" she asked. "They're nice, aren't they?"

"They sure are," Anne said, sipping at her drink. She liked the way things were turning out, and she could feel her pussy starting to get wet.

Catherine looked at her over the rim of her glass. "I have a lot more chains at home," she said.

Anne was feeling weak by now. "I'd like to see them sometime," she said quietly.

Catherine reached across the table and carefully took a lock of Anne's long brown hair between her fingers. "Let's not sit and talk all night," she said. She began to twist the hair around her hand. "I think you're lovely, and I want you. I want to take you home with me and show you my chains. I think you'd like that. I think you'd like to be tied up, and have me make love to you." She paused a moment. "I'm right, aren't I?"

Was she! Anne was almost dizzy at the thought of being chained and at this woman's mercy. She nodded, and Catherine smiled knowingly. Anne squirmed on the hard wooden seat to relieve her burning pussy.

Catherine was very satisfied with her guess. "I thought so," she said. "Your cute little pussy's just dying to be worked over, isn't it?" Anne nodded again. "Then let's go see what we can do about that."

They finished their drinks and left the bar. Anne had come by taxi, but Catherine had arrived by a much more interesting means. Her huge Harley-Davidson decker sat outside and she took Anne's hand and led her over to it.

"Pretty impressive," Anne said.

"Yeah, it is nice, isn't it?" Catherine said, with obvious pride. "I've put a lot of work into it." It was painted a rich, deep purple and the chrome had been polished until it reflected like a mirror. Catherine handed over a helmet, which Anne put on, and then indicated how to climb up behind her on the seat.

The engine roared into life. Anne had never been on a bike that big before. She could feel the throbbing through the leather seat, right into her pussy that was already damp with anticipation.

They took off down the road. Anne's long hair streamed behind her and the bike's hard seat felt so good against her cunt. She began to understand the fascination Catherine had with the huge, powerful machine between her legs. She sat close to Catherine, and the warm, musky leather smell of her jacket sent a whisper-light chill through her. She looked down and saw the chains on Catherine's boots. She could almost feel chains on her wrists, on her ankles, binding her firmly and leaving her at her lover's mercy. She was torn between the pleasure of riding the motorcycle and the desire to be at Catherine's house in her bedroom.

Catherine lived a couple of miles from the bar, in a small house in a quiet neighborhood. Anne was surprised at how ordinary and domestic the area was, and she wondered what the neighbors made of this tall woman with her leather clothes and big motorcycle. She wondered what they would think if they only knew what was going to be happening inside very shortly. The garage door was open and Catherine drove the big bike inside.

Almost reluctantly Anne climbed off. On a warm night like this she would have been happy to sit behind Catherine and ride around right into the dawn. But there was more waiting for her inside, and she followed the tall woman into the house. There was no formality, no coffee in the living room and small talk beforehand. They were both as hot as they could possibly be, and Catherine took her straight into the bedroom.

Anne was surprised. On the way to Catherine's house, she had pictured a special sexual torture room, with chains hanging off the walls and all sorts of leather and metal devices. Instead, the room looked pretty much like any other as she stood in the doorway. The bed was very large and had a heavy brass headboard and foot, with spindles. The hardwood floor was polished to a high shine and there was a small braided mat beside the bed. The only other furniture were a large dresser and a pine nightstand, piled high with books.

Catherine was behind her, and suddenly Anne felt her strong hands reaching around her and cupping her breasts. Her fingers were lovely and warm through the thin fabric of Anne's shirt. Catherine played with her nipples, brushing her fingers over them and pinching them gently. Anne sighed. Her pussy was throbbing again, and deliciously wet.

"Turn around," Catherine said. Anne did, and met the tall woman's kiss. She felt her shirt being unbuttoned as Catherine's tongue pressed between her teeth and teased her. Then Catherine pushed the shirt off her shoulders and onto the floor.

"You have beautiful tits," Catherine whispered, and ran her hands over them. She then strayed down and unbuttoned Anne's slacks, letting them drop around her ankles. Anne was wearing black lace panties, and Catherine put her hand between her legs.

"Your pussy is so wet," she said, pushing Anne's hair back and kissing her neck. "You want this, don't you?"

"Yes," Anne whispered.

"I'm going to tie you to that bed so you can't move," Catherine promised. Anne felt her knees go weak. "You won't be able to do anything except lie back and let me do whatever I want. You want to be chained up, don't you? You want to be tied and maybe even gagged, right?"

"Oh, yes!" Anne whispered, and returned Catherine's probing kiss. "Yes, yes!"

Catherine led her over to the bed and made her sit down on it. Then she opened the deep drawer in the nightstand. Anne's eyes widened with delight. The drawer was crammed full of leather straps, handcuffs, and rope. Anne realized that she had definitely underestimated Catherine's bedroom, which had looked so ordinary at first glance and which was quickly turning into the secret garden of delights she had so longed for this night.

Catherine looked through the drawer, and finally decided on two pairs of gleaming chrome handcuffs. Anne felt her pussy throb as they were snapped around her wrists. Then Catherine made her lie on the bed, and the other ends were closed around the headboard spindles. She was helpless and both of them knew it.

Slowly Catherine took off her clothes. Anne's eyes never left her body. The heavy leather motorcycle jacket was unzipped and left on the floor. Catherine's breasts were large and heavy, with hard nipples that Anne longed to suck on. The boots, with the chains that Anne admired so much, were discarded as well. Then she unzipped the black leather pants, revealing black underwear. Once they were off, Anne's mouth watered at the sight of Catherine's luscious mound. She wanted to taste it so badly.

Catherine got on the bed beside Anne and reached down to kiss her. Their tongues mingled and Catherine ran her hands slowly down her captive's body. Anne wanted to touch Catherine as well, but she was firmly shackled to the brass bed. When she pulled on the handcuffs, the steel bit into her wrists. She relaxed and returned Catherine's kiss.

The tall woman inched her way down to Anne's breasts. She was very slow and careful as she licked and sucked on the nipples and twisted them with her fingers. Anne moaned. Her pussy was already hot, and she felt each touch of Catherine's tongue on her nipples as a sweltering ripple in her cunt.

Then Catherine bent over so that her tits were in Anne's face. Anne sucked them into her mouth happily. She held the hard nub of nipple gently between her teeth and flicked her tongue over them, then sucked into her mouth as much of Catherine's breast as she could.

Then just as suddenly, Catherine pulled away. "You do that well," she said. "But we have all night." Anne tried to reach for her, to pull her back, but the cruel handcuffs wouldn't let her move.

Catherine moved down on the big bed and positioned herself between Anne's legs. "I'll bet your pussy's just waiting for me, isn't it?" she asked. Anne nodded.

Catherine licked her right through her thin panties, and Anne moaned. The first hot touch of the tall woman's tongue sent a thrill right through her whole body. She pushed her hips up for more.

Catherine's tongue traced a line up Anne's inner thigh. Then, with the very tip, she pushed the thin panties back and licked the hot hairy lips underneath. She did this on both sides, leaving Anne's steamy hole and clit untouched. Anne groaned, and bent her knees so that she could move her pussy in front of Catherine's mouth.

Catherine glared at her. "You were supposed to lie still," she admonished. "I trusted that you would, but now I know you won't. I'll have to fix that."

Slowly she pulled Anne's panties off of her, taking a moment to run her finger quickly and lightly over the exposed clit. Anne sighed. Then Catherine was back in the nightstand drawer, searching for a suitable device.

She came back with two leather straps. She buckled one around each of Anne's ankles and stretched her legs apart. Then, with two large chrome clasps she firmly secured Anne's legs to the foot of the bed. Anne was now spread-eagled on the bed, her wrists contained in handcuffs, her feet bound in leather straps, unable to move.

Satisfied with her work, Catherine went back to her position between Anne's shackled legs. She was maddeningly slow and knew how badly her captive wanted her touch. It wouldn't hurt to make her wait just a little while longer.

She licked all around Anne's wet pussy. Helpless on the bed, Anne thought she would go crazy waiting for a touch on her clit. She longed to reach down and push Catherine's head between her legs, to put that hot tongue right where she wanted it and hold it there until she came. But the strong cuffs held her back.

Catherine continued her slow torture. Then she slowly slid her finger into Anne's wet, tight hole. Anne groaned, and then almost cried out as she felt the first hot sweep of Catherine's tongue on her swollen clit.

It was like liquid fire seething up through her belly. Catherine knew exactly where to put her tongue, and she flicked over the most sensitive areas for a long time until Anne was on the edge of coming. Then she would glide away and leave Anne smoldering and drum-tight, begging for more.

She kept this up for some time, Constantly bringing Anne close and then letting her slide back before concentrating her efforts again. Then she stopped completely. Anne tried to push herself up, to be closer to her and to beg for more, but her heavy bonds wouldn't let her move.

To her joy, though, Catherine moved up beside her. "You want to taste my pussy, don't you?"

"Oh, please, yes!" Anne begged. She got her wish immediately, as Catherine knelt over her.

Catherine was just as excited as she was. Her pussy was hot and wet and Anne quickly applied her tongue to it. Her salty-sweet juice was combined with a faint, warm odor from the leather she had worn. Anne breathed deeply to savor it. She was no slouch herself at eating pussy and she flicked hard over Catherine's clit. Without thinking, she tried to touch her sweet cunt and slip a finger inside. The handcuffs immediately sent out a painful but wonderfully exciting reminder.

She obeyed Catherine's commands, lapping slowly the length of her cunt when told to, pushing hard against her clit at other times. Catherine controlled her completely, grinding her pussy down at times, moving her hips so that she slid on Anne's tongue, or even pulling away for long moments while Anne waited desperately for the hot, wet flesh to come back to her.

Finally she came back, and Anne licked her juicy cunt for all she was worth. Her face was wet with Catherine's honey, and the smell of her sex was everywhere. Anne loved it, and lapped at her hard.

Catherine came noisily, rubbing her pussy against Anne's outstretched tongue until she was finally finished. "You're very good," she said, and stroked Anne's cheek. "Your poor little pussy probably wants the same thing." Anne nodded.

Once again she felt Catherine's firm tongue on her pussy, and she moaned at how good it felt. Catherine was all business now. She pushed her tongue in Anne's hole, and then flicked it up and pushed her clit with the tip. Anne felt like she was falling into her orgasm. Catherine sucked her clit as she came. She tried to squirm but the bonds held her firm and her excitement increased even more. When it was finally over she was wet with sweat.

Catherine stretched out beside her and gently kissed her, then soothingly ran her hand up and down her body. Finally, when Anne had calmed down from her orgasm and was completely relaxed, Catherine went to the foot of the bed and took the leather straps off her ankles. Anne gratefully bent her stiff knees, then moved her cramped legs back and forth. Then the handcuffs came off, and she rubbed her tender wrists. The red marks in her skin still excited her.

Catherine led her to the kitchen, where she made mugs of hot tea for both of them. They sat at the table sipping them.

"I'd really like it if you'd stay the night," Catherine said, and Anne agreed. It was late when they finished their drinks and they went back into the bedroom. There, Catherine buckled a leather strap around one of Anne's wrists and locked it to the bed. It was a symbolic gesture only, for Anne could easily have reached up and opened it, but the thought of being chained to this stranger's bed all night excited her immensely. Both of them knew she would still be locked onto it in the morning.

Catherine fell asleep hugged up tightly to her, and within moments of hearing her steady, shallow breathing, Anne fell asleep too. When she woke up, Catherine was already moving around the house as Anne was still getting her bearings.

She came into the bedroom, fully dressed, and took the strap off Anne's wrist. "I've called a taxi for you," she said. "I have to go to work today. You'd better get dressed."

She did. Her arm was cramped from lying in one

position all night, but her pussy still felt wonderfully satisfied from the previous night's session. When she went into the kitchen, Catherine had a mug of coffee waiting for her, and she drank it while waiting for her cab.

She saw the car pull up in front of the house. Catherine asked her where she was going, then pressed money into her hand to cover the fare. "I'm usually at the bar in the evenings," she said. "You might want to come back in and see me."

She kissed her deeply, then led her out of the house and locked the door behind them. Anne got into the taxi and told the driver her destination. As the car pulled away, she looked out the back window and got a glimpse of Catherine driving off in the opposite direction on the huge purple Harley.

She didn't go home, but decided to go to the mall near her apartment and do some shopping. She stopped for breakfast in the mall restaurant first and sat by herself at the window. The early summer sun was very bright and she basked in its warmth as it streamed through the glass. When she reached for her toast, the bright light showed up the angry red marks left on her wrists by the chrome handcuffs. The whole beautiful evening came back to her vividly as she rubbed her wrists carefully.

Throughout the morning she was reminded of Catherine constantly. Her arm was still sore from being shackled to the bed all night, but she relished the pain. Her ankles felt a bit raw from the heavy leather straps. When she tried on a shirt, the sales clerk adjusted the sleeves, and Anne could see that she was looking at the marks on her wrists with a puzzled expression. It pleased her no end, and she wondered if the clerk would ever know exactly what had caused them.

Walking past a shoe store, she glanced into the window and stopped dead. Right at the back of the display was a pair of expensive snakeskin cowboy boots, and slung around the ankles were decorative silver chains. She remembered the sound that Catherine's made and the way they were wrapped so tightly.

She went back to the bar on Monday night. To her pleasure, she saw the big Harley parked outside. The place was almost empty, and Catherine spotted her right away, motioning for her to sit down in the booth.

"I thought you weren't coming back," she said, motioning for the waitress to bring Anne a drink.

"I had plans I'd made a long time ago," Anne explained. "I couldn't get out of them."

Catherine reached across the table and stroked her cheek. "I've been thinking about you," she said. "I was really hoping I'd see you again."

The Manhattan arrived and Anne sipped at it. She noticed that Catherine was wearing a heavy, chain-link gold bracelet as well as the chains on her boots. She was thrilled. Everything about the woman reminded her of being helpless and shackled on the bed. She had never met anyone this powerful before.

Even Catherine's leather clothes turned her on again. Her pussy grew very warm. The black leather reminded Anne of the strap she had worn through the night, the strap that made her Catherine's property and bound her to the bed where they had enjoyed their wild sex.

Once again, Catherine was straight to the point, all business. When they finished their drinks, she paid the bill and led Anne outside. As before, they both climbed on the big bike and rumbled onto the street.

It was still fairly early and many of Catherine's

neighbors were outside. Anne still couldn't picture Catherine living in this neighborhood, where people were cutting the grass or sitting on the porch, and children were playing or riding their bicycles. Except for the motorcycle in the garage, Catherine's house looked the same as any other, with its neatly-trimmed lawn, geraniums in the flowerbed and curtains in the window. She didn't think any of the neighbors could ever dream about the wild sex scenes that took place in Catherine's bedroom, its dresser drawer jammed with handcuffs and straps. She finally realized that this was probably the whole idea behind the small, well-kept bungalow.

Catherine parked the motorcycle, closed the garage door, and unlocked the door that led into the house. This time, though, they passed by Catherine's bedroom entirely. She led Anne down the hall to another door.

This opened onto a second bedroom, but it was considerably different from Catherine's modest sleeping area. Anne's eyes opened wide as she looked around. The room was almost empty, except for a plain daybed heaped with pillows and a chair.

The walls were what fascinated her. It seemed that Catherine had a secret torture room after all. At several spots there were heavy metal rings screwed into the white paneling, all at various heights. Some were close to the floor while others were further up on the walls than Anne could reach. There were even four of them screwed into the ceiling.

One of the pairs of rings, almost at Anne's eye level, had short chains attached to them. Dangling from the chains were a pair of leather straps similar to the ones she had worn all night. She sucked in her breath. Below them, almost at the floor, were two more rings, with the same chains. The heavy leather straps lay open and inviting on the carpet.

Catherine closed the door behind them and moved to face Anne. She kissed her hard and slipped her tongue inside her captive's mouth. Anne returned the kiss, shyly at first and then with increasing excitement. She once again felt herself slipping helplessly under Catherine's powerful spell.

The tall woman undressed her quickly and led her to the wall. She positioned her so that her back was to the wall and expertly buckled the straps on her wrists and ankles.

Anne was almost beside herself with desire. Her arms were stretched out on either side of her, and she was firmly shackled so that she could hardly move. The rings holding her ankles were far enough apart that her legs were spread and her wet pussy was exposed and waiting for Catherine's touch. The wall was hard and cool behind her. Her discomfort only added to her excitement. She wondered what Catherine had in store for her.

Catherine was meanwhile doing a slow striptease in front of her. She unzipped the heavy motorcycle jacket and tossed it on the floor. Her large breasts were held in a supple black leather bra with holes cut out so that her large nipples showed through. Just as slowly she unfastened the leather pants, and stuck her hand inside to feel her own pussy. "That's for you," she promised, and Anne's tongue pressed against her teeth, desperately wanting a taste of it. Under the leather jeans, Catherine was wearing soft leather panties that matched the bra.

She stepped over to Anne and kissed her. As she did, she reached down and took Anne's breasts into her hands, cupping and kneading them. Anne groaned and returned her kiss. Every now and again

Catherine would step back and break off the kiss, then return a few moments later. Anne was helpless and could only wait for her to return. The straps kept her firmly chained to the wall and Catherine took every opportunity to remind her of it.

"Lick my tits," Catherine said, and stood straight before her. She was tall enough that Anne had only to bend her head down to reach the breast that Catherine put in front of her.

She sucked the nipple into her mouth. The leather bra tasted musky and stale in her mouth but she loved it. Catherine's nipple was firm and she could feel it growing harder and bigger between her lips. Catherine moved back and forth, feeding her one nipple and then the other. Sometimes she would step back and Anne would be cruelly reminded of her bondage before the hot nipples were given back to her.

Catherine then knelt on the floor before her. Anne's legs were already spread wide by the unforgiving straps and she moaned as she felt Catherine's hot, wet tongue part her pussy lips and slide over her clit.

Catherine's tongue danced over her. Anne wanted to move, to push that probing tongue deeper, but she could only stand ramrod-straight against the wall, her wrists hanging in the straps.

Hot thrills went up and down Anne's spine as Catherine licked her. Anne could feel hot juice on her legs and she knew her pussy was soaked. Her legs felt weak, but there was no relief from her chains. She closed her eyes and enjoyed the attention her pussy was receiving.

Catherine then stopped and stood up. Anne moaned. She had been so close to coming! But Catherine just held her tits and kissed her, seemingly oblivious to Anne's agony. Anne could taste her own pussy on Catherine's tongue, and she kissed her hard. The hot smell of her cunt seemed to be everywhere.

Then Catherine abruptly turned and walked out of the room, closing the door behind her. Anne was completely confused and struggled in her bonds, which of course didn't budge.

She waited for several minutes. Her arms had gone numb but she barely felt her discomfort. Her eyes were glued to the door, waiting for Catherine to return.

The door finally opened, and Anne's eyes went wide in surprise. The leather underwear set was gone. Instead, Catherine wore a harness strapped firmly around her hips. At the front was a large curved dildo sticking out of it.

Catherine closed the door behind her and walked toward Anne. "It's a nice big one, isn't it?" she crooned. Her hand stroked the head as if she were masturbating. "I want to fuck you with it."

She hugged Anne's neck and kissed her hard. Anne felt the dildo between them, the head pressed against her belly. It was warm, as if it had been dipped in hot water, and was made of supple rubber that felt almost like flesh. Still with her mouth on Anne's, Catherine swung her hips so that the dildo stroked them both. Then she reached down and put the head at Anne's pussy lips.

The lips were pushed aside and Anne felt the head in her cunt. She groaned and pushed her tongue in Catherine's mouth. Slowly the dildo slid into her. She felt deliciously full.

"Do you like my dick in you?" Catherine whispered. She slowly stroked it in and out of Anne's sopping pussy. "I've got a beautiful big dick, haven't I?"

"Yes!" Anne whispered. Catherine was kissing her neck, her face, her lips. The dildo was sliding in faster and faster. Catherine was kissing her neck, her face, her lips. The dildo was sliding in faster and faster. Catherine reached down and slipped her hand between them so that her fingers were on Anne's clit. Anne moaned as she felt her hot button being massaged.

Catherine was fucking her hard now. The rubber cock banged into her again and again. With each thrust, Anne felt Catherine's fingers rub her clit. There was nothing else in the world except her pussy. She wanted Anne to push the dildo in her up to its root. "Fuck me faster!" she gasped. "Oh yes, harder! Fuck me!"

Her ass was being pounded into the wall. The dildo went deep again and again and Catherine's fingers groped hard at her clit.

She came so violently she thought she would pass out. With the dildo inside her she tensed up and felt the burning flood go through her body. She all but screamed as the final throbs tore at her and she hung from her chains limply, completely drained. She would have fallen if her shackles hadn't held her up.

Catherine stepped back, sliding the dildo out of Anne's pussy. It was wet and glistening. She unbuckled the straps holding Anne's wrists. Anne's legs were too weak to support her and Catherine held her tightly, lowering her gently to the carpet until she was stretched out on her stomach. She remained shackled to the wall by her legs.

Anne sobbed as the feeling returned to her numb arms in painful swells. The agony mingled deliciously with the sweet satisfaction in her pussy. Catherine waited until she had enough strength back in her arms to lift herself up on her elbows.

She then sat on the carpet in front of Anne, her legs stretched out on either side of her. The dildo stood up defiantly from its harness. "Suck my cock!" Catherine ordered. "Suck it hard!"

Anne took the rubber dildo into her mouth. Her sweet pussy juice was all over it. She licked the head, then sucked it in deeply. Catherine watched her with a smile on her face. She loved having a woman captive and bound in front of her as much as Anne loved the feeling of ropes and chains around her wrists.

She let Anne lick and suck the cock for quite a while. Then she leaned back and unstrapped the harness. It was tossed onto the chair and Catherine stretched out on the floor, her pussy in front of Anne's face. She was just far enough away that Anne had to stretch out, the chains on her ankles holding her back. She could feel the constant pressure on her feet, a reminder that she was still very firmly under Catherine's domination.

Catherine's pussy was as wet as Anne's had been. Anne licked it eagerly, savoring the hot, wine-rich taste. Catherine held her head firmly as she sucked at the tall woman's cunt. The shackles held Anne firmly to the wall.

She used the tip of her tongue to stroke Catherine's clit, then lapped hard up and down her whole pussy. Catherine moaned. She flicked the swollen clit back and forth, faster and faster.

Catherine groaned loudly as she came, her whole body shivering. Just as she began to calm down, Anne licked her hard several times, sending rich spasms through her and prolonging the wonderful sensations.

Catherine finally got up and unbuckled the straps holding Anne's ankles. It felt so good to move her legs and bend her knees. They hugged each other, lying on the thickly carpeted floor. It felt so good to kiss and caress.

Catherine asked her if she could stay the night again, and Anne quickly agreed. It was dark outside but still warm, and Catherine got two bottles of beer out of the refrigerator and led Anne outside to the patio in the back yard.

It felt very strange to Anne, sitting in the lawn chair talking and drinking beer as if she were visiting her family at home. The quiet domestic setting was totally at odds with the Catherine who had shackled her firmly to the wall and fucked her so completely. It was like a completely different world outside the little house.

Catherine even waved to her neighbors next door when they came out to sit on their own patio. Anne felt an odd sensation go through her. She didn't know if it was pride or the fact that she knew a forbidden secret that the neighbors on the street would never be able to guess. The neighbors saw a neat house with a manicured lawn and a nicely kept flower garden. Anne knew a drawer filled with strange devices, and a room with rings on the walls and chains that dangled from them and held women tight.

The strange feeling passed quickly enough when Catherine decided it was time for bed, and they went back into the house. She would not let Anne undress herself, but insisted on doing it as Anne stood in the hallway just outside the bedroom.

Anne looked inside and saw the familiar brass bed. Then she noticed a chain firmly locked on it, and a leather strap waiting for her on the pillow. Her pussy stirred and she returned Catherine's kiss passionately. She could hardly wait.

MISTRESS' ORDERS

I heard the familiar hiss just before the riding crop landed on my bare ass. I knew it was coming, I knew how it would burn a welt into my pale skin, but it still caught me totally by surprise. My Mistress had a way of doing that.

"Stupid slave!" she said again and again, and each time the crop punctuated her words. Within moments I was sobbing and my ass was burning hot. No matter what, I knew I would never do that again.

"That" was the horrible crime of upsetting half a bucket of soapy water on the kitchen floor. I had been ordered to scrub it on my hands and knees with a small scrub brush. Somehow I had turned around too quickly and had bumped the bucket with my elbow. That was enough to knock it over, and enough to set off my Mistress' temper.

"Now finish your job, and don't fuck up again!" she hissed. I started to get up, but the crop slammed into my back. "You don't walk again until I tell you it's permissible," she said. "If you need anything, you crawl."

It wasn't easy crawling with the bucket in front of me, and I had to go all the way to the bathroom since the faucet in the tub would be the only one I would be able to reach from my knees. But my Mistress had ordered it, and that was what I would have to do.

I had been coming to my Mistress' penthouse apartment for six months. I met her when she placed an advertisement in the personals column of a local paper. I had answered it and was given her address. When I arrived, the sweet voice on the intercom invited me to come upstairs.

It was much different once I found myself in front of her apartment door. She opened it about an inch, and ordered me to strip off all of my clothes, standing there in the hallway. I'd never done anything like that before, but there was a steely strength in her voice that told me refusal would be very foolish. I dropped my clothes right there, got on all fours as she ordered, and finally crawled inside the apartment. I had been coming back regularly ever since.

I finally made my way up the long hallway to the bathroom, and slipped the bucket under the faucet. I filled it up and then discovered that getting to the bathroom had been the easy part. Getting the heavy bucket back to the kitchen without spilling any was going to take a tremendous amount of work.

I eventually did it by sliding the bucket forward an inch at a time, praying that the suds wouldn't splash out over the top. It seemed to take forever, but I got back to the kitchen and continued scrubbing. My knees were killing me but there was nothing I could do. Mistress had ordered it, and I would obey.

"Alicia!"

"Yes, Mistress?" I replied.

"Alicia, hurry up with that floor." She appeared in the doorway. As always, she was magnificent. She was wearing a black corset and matching panties, and her long beautiful legs were clad in black fishnet stocking. Her heels were impossibly high. The leather riding crop was still in her hand. "Mistress Lorna will be here very shortly, and I don't want you still cleaning up."

"Yes, Mistress," I said, and scrubbed faster. Mistress Lorna was one of her lovers—just how many she had, I didn't know. She had other slaves as well, for I'd often seen coarse clothes and shackles that I'd never worn. But I had never met them, and I knew better than to ask.

I was finally finished. My Mistress gave me permission to stand up, and I did so stiffly. Everything was ready. There was a bottle of fine champagne chilling in the refrigerator, along with the expensive hors d'oeuvres that the catering company had dropped off earlier in the day. The apartment was spotless.

"Go and clean yourself up," she ordered. I did so gratefully. The shower was hot and I could have stood under it all day, but I knew better. I soaped myself quickly, washed my hair and got out. Keeping my Mistress waiting was not a good idea.

I dried myself off. My Mistress was waiting in her bedroom for me. She combed my hair and dried it. I was spritzed with perfume, and a tiny touch of rouge was dabbed on my nipples to bring out their color. I was given a pair of tiny lace panties to put on. My costume was complete when my Mistress buckled a wide leather dog collar around my neck. It hung a bit loosely, heavy with metal studs. I loved the feeling of it around my throat. She often put it on me and snapped a leash on, making me walk around the apartment, sometimes on my feet, sometimes on my hands and knees.

She was just finishing up when the intercom buzzer rang. "Go wait in the living room, Alicia," she said, as she went to answer it.

I knew my position from past experience. There was a corner, empty of any furniture, and I got on my knees, my back straight and my hands on my thighs.

I heard her greet Mistress Lorna at the door, and soon afterward they both came into the living room. I had been in Mistress Lorna's presence once before. She was a tall black woman, beautifully built and with an icy, cold stare that sent shivers down my spine. She was dressed in a tight leather miniskirt and a shirt that showed off her hard nipples.

They sat down on the sofa. Mistress Lorna glanced over at me, but her expression didn't change. It was as if I were just another piece of furniture in the room. She talked to my Mistress casually about the traffic outside and how warm it was. Neither of them seemed to notice that there was a woman, almost naked and wearing a dog's collar, sitting on the floor in front of them.

Finally my Mistress looked over in my direction. "Alicia, we'll have some champagne now," she said. "And bring out the tray of food."

"Yes, Mistress," I said, and hurried to fulfill her orders. The champagne was very cold and I eased the cork out of the bottle, then poured two glasses and set them on a silver tray. I took it to them. They each took a glass without even glancing at me.

I returned to the kitchen, put the bottle back in the refrigerator, and took out the box containing the hors d'oeuvres. They were exquisite. There were toast rounds with caviar, little sausage rolls, shrimp in puff pastry cases and tiny tarts filled with curried chicken and pine nuts. I was hungry, and the sight of the tray made my mouth water. I knew better than to touch one, though. My ass was still tender from my lesson over the water bucket.

I set the tray down on the table and hurried back to my corner. My Mistress stopped me. "Alicia," she said, "come back and sit at the table."

I knelt down before the table, the tray of food in front of me. They ignored me, sipping their champagne and taking the tidbits between their long, painted fingernails. I wanted a treat badly and I couldn't help staring at them.

My Mistress took a bite of her sausage roll, then held the other half out to me, like she was feeding a dog. I couldn't resist and snatched it from her fingers with my teeth.

What a mistake! Immediately my Mistress slapped my face hard. I blinked away tears and hung my head.

"You know better than that!" she hissed. My cheek was burning and I knew it was bright red. "You've been taught to take food properly!"

"I'm sorry, Mistress," I said. "I should have known better. I was hungry and I forgot what I was doing."

Her voice became a bit softer, the mockery of a concerned parent. "Of course you're hungry," she said. "You've been working all day with nothing to eat. Come here, my little slave."

I did. My Mistress gave me a curry tart and then a round of the black caviar. They were delicious, but shortly after I ate them, I realized that her kindness had been a cruel trap. The salt had parched my throat and I was dreadfully thirsty.

"Please, Mistress," I begged, "may I have a drink?"

She had been in mid-sentence, speaking with Mistress Lorna. I saw her hand raise, but she moved so quickly I didn't have time to flinch. Again her hand struck my cheek hard, knocking me over. I knew better than to get up.

"Stupid slave!" she cried. "How dare you interrupt me when I'm speaking! Not only will you get no water but you can stay on the floor like that until we're ready for you."

They both carried on just as calmly as before. Neither of them even glanced at me, lying on the floor on my side, tears streaming from my eyes. I watched them intently. Even when she was cruel to me, I couldn't take my eyes off my beautiful Mistress.

My Mistress reached across and took Mistress Lorna's champagne glass out of her hand, setting it on the table. She then leaned over and kissed Mistress Lorna's full, luscious lips. My tongue licked my own lips. I wanted to be kissed by my Mistress like that.

They didn't even acknowledge that there was a third person in the room. I was only a slave and of no more account than the table or the carpet. I watched them, but stayed down; I still hadn't been given permission to get up.

My Mistress leaned back as Mistress Lorna rubbed her tits through her black corset. They kissed again, and then Mistress Lorna licked and sucked at her nipples which stuck out just over the tops of her lace cups. Kneeling on the carpet, she removed my Mistress' panties.

I saw my Mistress' beautiful cunt as she spread her legs open and leaned back into the cushions. Mistress Lorna took the place I longed to be in, right in front of that hot, steamy mound. She began to lick my Mistress' clit. My mouth was watering, my thirst forgotten, as I watched her. I desperately wanted to do it for her instead.

She licked slowly, until my Mistress told her she wanted it faster and harder. Immediately Mistress Lorna's tongue was dancing like wildfire over my Mistress' clit. I was insanely jealous, but there was nothing I could do but lie on the floor and obey my Mistress' command to stay where her blow had sent me.

My Mistress came very quickly. She did not cry out, but I saw her muscles tense and her legs quiver in the way I knew well. She pulled her panties back up, and as Mistress Lorna returned to the sofa beside her, she picked up her champagne glass and took a sip. Her eyes fell on me.

"Oh, the slave," she said. "I had forgotten about you. You may sit up now."

I did. "Thank you, Mistress."

Daintily my Mistress took a shrimp tidbit. This time I got none. "Did you bring it?" she asked Mistress Lorna.

"Of course," the black woman replied. She looked at me over the rim of her champagne glass. I dropped my eyes. Although she wasn't my Mistress, she was a dominatrix too and commanded the same respect. Only a command from my own Mistress could override any order from her. I had learned that lesson the first time I had met her. I had failed to treat her with the proper respect. My Mistress had bound me, strapped a rubber ball gag in my mouth, and beaten me thoroughly with her riding crop, allowing Mistress Lorna the privilege of a few hard strokes of her own.

Mistress Lorna reached into her purse. My eyes opened wide as she brought out a long, dildo-shaped vibrator and handed it to my Mistress.

"Take your panties off," my Mistress ordered.

I did. Mistress Lorna looked at me and said, "Oh you found yourself a cute little one." My Mistress smiled.

My Mistress turned the dial on the bottom of the device and the vibrator hummed. She held it between her hands, then ran it over her neck. "Good," she said. "This will do just fine."

To my horror, she handed the vibrator over the table to me. It was still humming and the vibrations ran through my hands. My Mistress smiled. "Use it," she said.

I looked at her puzzled. "Mistress?"

"You heard me," she said coldly. "Use it."

Slowly I moved the vibrator between my legs. I was still kneeling on the floor.

"Not that way," my Mistress said. "Lie on your back. We want to see just what you're doing."

My face was burning with shame as I stretched out on the carpet. Certainly I had masturbated before—I did it every time I went home after visiting my Mistress. But I had never done such a thing in front of anyone else. It had always been a private act for me. Now I was being forced to submit to the pleasures of a battery-operated machine while lying on the floor before my Mistress and her guest.

"We'd appreciate it if this could be accomplished today," my Mistress said sarcastically. "Or would you prefer using it with the riding crop stuffed up your ass too?"

"No, Mistress," I whispered. I put the humming vibrator to my pussy and closed my eyes.

Despite my embarrassment, the vibrator felt good on my clit. I always enjoyed making myself come, because no one knew the sensitive spots better than I did. The humiliation of doing it solely because my mistress had commanded me to heightened my excitement more than I thought it would. She knew it, too; in fact, she knew all the right buttons to push. She had not been the first dominatrix I had known, but she was definitely the best.

"Open your eyes," my Mistress said. I did. They were still drinking their champagne and eating the hors d'oeuvres. They did not watch me all the time, but occasionally looked over during their conversation.

I couldn't help myself. The vibrator felt so good, and I began pushing it hard against my clit and moving it back and forth. I was so close to coming. My hips moved up and down, grinding the humming wand deeper. I was breathing heavily, relishing the warmth in my wet pussy.

"Alicia," my Mistress said, "Mistress Lorna's glass is empty. Bring us more champagne.

I could hardly believe it. I was so close to slipping into a huge orgasm! But there would be a terrible penalty for ignoring my Mistress' command. I turned the vibrator off and got up. I waited while my Mistress drained her glass and carried them both into the kitchen.

My breath was coming in sobs. My pussy was throbbing and my whole belly felt tight and unfulfilled. I took clean glasses from the cupboard and uncorked the bottle. It seemed to take forever for the rush of bubbles to subside so that I could finish filling the glasses. Every second I spent in that kitchen was a moment away from the delicious vibrator.

I put the glasses on the silver tray and carried them back to the two women on the sofa. They took them, and I returned the tray to the kitchen, then went back and stood before my Mistress.

"Well, what are you waiting for?" she asked. "Go back to what you were doing."

This time I was so hot, there was no shame. I got back on the floor and turned the dial on that wonderful little device. I didn't care that they were enjoying my humiliation. All that mattered was the liquid fire in my pussy that the vibrator was stoking.

I came so violently I thought I would push the vibrator right through my clit. My legs shook and my hips bucked wildly. I felt dizzy with the rush that flowed through me, and when I finally turned the vibrator off it was soaked with my pussy juice. My whole body was covered with sweat.

"How was that, Alicia?" my Mistress asked in a buttery-smooth voice.

"Oh, wonderful, Mistress!" I said. "Thank you, Mistress. Thank you, Mistress Lorna."

"She's worked up quite a sweat," Mistress Lorna observed.

"You're right," my Mistress said. "I'd better take care of that. I don't want her getting sick or anything. I'll let her cool off."

My Mistress told me to sit up. Then she went into the bedroom and returned with a heavy leather dog leash. She snapped one end of it to the ring in my studded collar. Then she made me get up, and led me to the door that opened onto her balcony.

My knees went weak as I realized what she was going to do. "Mistress, no!" I begged. That earned me another slap on my cheek, and I kept silent. Tears were running down my face as I prepared for one of my most basic fears.

She opened the door and brazenly led me out on the balcony. We were on the top floor, but the balcony had glass walls, and anyone looking over from another penthouse would be able to see me. She tied the leash to the metal railing just above the glass. I could not reach the door, and had to remain close to the clear glass wall.

My Mistress went back into the apartment and closed the door firmly behind her. I was trapped. I curled up into a ball. It was very warm outside, and I was not uncomfortable, but it went through my mind that the nice sunny weather might make other people think about sitting on their own balconies. I looked around. No one else was out, but I was still terrified.

I could easily have untied the leash and cringed against the door, but that was out of the question. My Mistress had tied me here, and I would have to stay here until she decided it was time to take me inside. Her word was law. If she decided to leave me out all night, then I would just have to sleep curled up against the glass.

At one point she must have remembered my thirst, for she came outside—a heavy satin robe over her corset—and brought me a glass of water. I drank gratefully while she held the glass as if for a child. I thanked her, but did not ask to be let back in. It was her decision. She closed the door behind her.

I had one close call, when a neighbor decided to come out on his own balcony. I hear the door and looked over, horrified, as a man walked to the railing and took in the view below. But he never looked over, and to my immense relief, he finally went back inside. My heart beat so hard my whole body shook.

Finally, an eternity later, my Mistress came out and calmly untied the leash, then led me back inside. "Mistress Lorna has left," she said as she unsnapped it from my collar. "You may clean up now."

"Yes, Mistress," I said, and hurried to carry the trays and glasses back to the kitchen and wash them. When I was finished, she walked into the kitchen and threw my clothes on the floor. "Leave now," she said.

I dressed quickly, then stood by the door. I knew I

had to wait, without calling for her, until she was ready for me. She took a long time before walking over and unbuckling the collar from around my neck. "Thank you, Mistress," I whispered.

"I will send for you," she said, and I walked out into the hall. The door closed behind me.

All the way home I watched the people on the bus, like a child with an enormous secret. No one would ever suspect that the small, ordinary-looking woman in their midst had spent her afternoon in a collar, her most private sexual act witnessed by two women who thought nothing of it. Would they understand why I craved the humiliation of being tied naked outside? Could they know that even now my pussy was burning with desire to be in that collar again, at the mercy of my Mistress? When I finally arrived home I was so excited that I tore off my clothes and used my own vibrator to give myself another shattering orgasm.

I received a note from my Mistress in the mail a few days later. I could tell it was from her right away, by the neat script and the crisp, heavy stationery, written with the costly fountain pen I had seen her use. Everything about her was classy and expensive.

The note was brief, consisting of a single order. Be at her apartment in two days, at two o'clock. There was no signature, no return address. I felt weak and wondered how I was going to get through those two days. I suffered through two sleepless nights and when I was finally ready to leave for her apartment, I had worked myself up into a sweet sexual frenzy.

My Mistress met me at the door to her apartment. She was dressed in a tight black bodysuit made of thin, supple leather, and she wore stiletto-heeled boots that came up over her knees. Her long dark hair curled about her face. She held her riding crop

in one hand and my dog collar in another. I breathed
hard. I could almost have come just at the sight of
her. I wanted to fall on the floor and lick her boots,
giving myself over to her completely.

She motioned for me to come inside. "Undress
yourself," she said, as she closed the door behind me.

I started to strip my clothes off, but I was so
eager I fumbled with the buttons on my shirt.
Immediately the riding crop slammed against my
ass. Tears sprang to my eyes and I could feel a welt
rising up. I hurried to get the shirt off, but taking
much more care this time. My Mistress seldom
repeated a punishment twice; if I didn't learn the
first time, I could count on a much more severe
reminder to follow.

When I was completely naked, the heavy dog collar was put around my neck and buckled into place. I
was instructed to follow my Mistress into the kitchen.
It was quickly obvious that this was the only piece of
clothing I was going to receive.

At her command, I knelt before her on the hard
kitchen floor. As always, it was spotless, and I wondered if another slave had been whipped while washing it as I had been. My hands on my knees, my head
bowed, I sat while my Mistress reached down and
toyed with a lock of my hair.

"This is a very special day, Alicia," she said. She
moved closer and I could smell her rich perfume and
the warm leather smell of her boots. "As a result, I
have some very special instructions for you. I want
you to listen carefully, for I will not repeat them."

"Yes, Mistress," I said.

"We have a guest today," she said, "a guest who
has brought an interesting playmate. You are not to
speak a single word to this playmate, under any cir-
cumstances. You are not to speak any words except

'Yes, Mistress,' or 'No, Mistress,' and you are only to speak when you are spoken to. Do you understand?"

"Yes, Mistress," I said. "I—"

Another mistake! Immediately I felt her fingers grab my collar and I was pulled roughly to my feet. "You stupid slave!" she said. "You can't follow even the simplest instructions! You need a lesson in discipline."

With that, she opened a drawer and pulled out two metal objects. I felt myself go cold as I realized they were nipple clamps. Within seconds she had snapped them shut on my tender flesh.

I knew screaming wouldn't be permitted, so I bit my tongue hard. My whole chest felt like the skin was being ripped off it. The cruel clamps twisted and burned. I knew from experience that they were a double-edged sword; it hurt as much to take them off as to put them on. I would pay dearly for my mistake not once, but twice.

She reached out and tapped one of the clamps with her finger. My stomach churned with the pain, but only a tiny groan escaped my lips.

"That's much better," she smiled. "No get to work. There's a bottle of champagne in the refrigerator. We will have two glasses in the living room." She turned on one incredibly high heel and left.

I struggled to uncork the bottle. Every movement of my arms seemed to make the clamps bite harder, and I had to stop and steady myself when a wave of nausea caused by the pain flashed through me. I poured the rich, wheat-colored wine and placed the glasses on the silver tray. I carried them very carefully, taking tiny steps so that my breasts didn't move and send more pain through me.

Mistress Lorna was seated on the sofa beside my Mistress. She was dressed in a luscious tight suit with cutouts for her large breasts. They stood out firmly with the nipples hard and inviting. But I had eyes only for my Mistress, who took her offered glass of champagne with her long, graceful fingers.

"Down on the floor, Alicia," my Mistress ordered once I had served Mistress Lorna. I put the tray on the table and then knelt before her.

"We have a surprise for you," Mistress Lorna said. "Come here, Sandra."

I could hardly believe it. A woman walked in from around the corner and swiftly knelt on the floor before Mistress Lorna. I stared, open-mouthed.

She was blonde, about my age, and she looked at me with the same puzzled interest. She was naked, wearing only a heavy chain around her neck and leather straps on her wrists that could quickly be snapped together to bind her. She looked at my breasts, with the unforgiving nipple clamps secured on them, and I felt my face grow red. No one but my Mistress and three of her dominatrix friends had ever seen me as a slave. I felt almost violated.

"This is Sandra," my Mistress said. "She belongs to Mistress Lorna. I am sure you two would have plenty to talk about, but she is under the same rule of silence that you are. You may not speak to each other, and you may not speak unless spoken to. If either of you breaks this rule, you will both be punished."

They sipped their champagne, then my Mistress snapped her fingers at me. "Come here, Alicia," she said. "On your hands and knees."

I did, then knelt before her. Roughly she tore the clamps off my nipples. I fought hard to keep from fainting. My flesh was burning hot and I was in agony.

"That must really hurt," my Mistress said.

"Sandra, come over here and make Alicia's nipples feel better."

"Yes, Mistress," the blonde woman said, and she crawled over on her hands and knees to me. I could hardly believe it when she tenderly took my sore tits in her hands and began to lick my nipples. The two women on the sofa sipped their drinks and looked on approvingly. This was a novelty for all of us and for once they were not ignoring me.

Her soft tongue did make my nipples feel better. I began to experience the hot stirrings in my pussy that I knew so well. The thought of being caressed by another slave, a woman I couldn't even speak to, while my Mistress and her lover watched was turning me on immensely. I could not have refused her touch. I was only a slave in my Mistress' command.

Sandra was obviously being turned on as well. She was now circling my nipples with her tongue and sucking on them, flicking her tongue over them rapidly. A soft moan escaped me. "That's it, Alicia," my Mistress said. "Let us know how good it feels." I gasped as the blonde woman nibbled gently on my sore nipple. The pain was as exquisite as the pleasure of her tongue.

"Don't be greedy," my Mistress said. "Share with Sandra. Show her what you can do."

The blonde woman sat up straight. Her nipples were huge and I sucked them into my mouth. I felt so strange making love to a woman I couldn't even speak to. She moaned as well as I worked her nipples over with my mouth.

"Sandra," Mistress Lorna said, "lie down on the floor. Do as I told you to."

"Yes, Mistress," Sandra whispered. I could see how uncomfortable she was, performing in front of them. She stretched out on her back.

"Now, Alicia," my Mistress said, "turn around and get on top of her."

My eyes widened as I realized what they expected us to do. I didn't move fast enough and within a second, the riding crop had smashed down twice across my shoulders. "I gave you an order, slave!" my Mistress hissed. "I don't expect to have to repeat it!"

"Yes, Mistress," I said. Carefully I positioned myself over the blonde woman, who looked just as embarrassed as I felt. My pussy was over her face, and her blonde mound was right below me.

I flicked my tongue over her pussy. She was hot and wet, and in that moment, I realized that I was too. This unique brand of domination was turning both of us on. I felt her hot tongue flash over my own clit and I moaned.

I couldn't help myself. It just felt so good, and within moments I was eating her cunt as joyfully as if it had been my Mistress'. Meanwhile her tongue was doing a number on my clit as well, and by the way she was moving her hips, I knew she was enjoying it too.

Everything I had was centered on the blonde woman's steamy pussy. The rich smell of her cunt was in my nose, my skin, my hair. Her thick sweet juice was all over my tongue and chin. I sucked on her clit and pushed a finger into her tight, hot hole. I continued to slide it in and out while I licked her.

She was just as occupied with me. I could feel pressure building up in my cunt as her tongue did a swift tap-dance over my clit. I licked her harder, and she responded by grinding her tongue into me.

I came first, and she followed me a few moments later. Both of us moaned loudly, our tongues still firmly in each other's cunts, our pussies pushed into each other's faces to get the very last rush of pleasure. Finally we both stopped, exhausted and satisfied.

My Mistress' voice quickly broke the spell. Indeed, I had been so involved with Sandra that I had almost forgotten where I was. "Alicia, you may get up now," she said.

"Yes, Mistress," I replied, and moved back into a kneeling position before her. At Mistress Lorna's command, Sandra did the same thing. We looked at each other, both breathing hard, our hair mussed and our lips glistening with pussy juice.

When Mistress Lorna finished her glass of champagne, she decided it was time to leave. She slipped a loose dress over her lovely suit and threw Sandra's clothes to her. I watched them go with a strange feeling in my chest. I had just shared one of the most intimate acts with this woman; I could still taste her pussy on my lips. But I had never spoken a word with her, and knew I would probably never see her again.

My Mistress closed the door, then turned to me and smiled. "I give you permission to speak, slave," she said. "Did you enjoy your little encounter?"

"Very much, Mistress," I said.

She lifted my chin with her fingers and looked into my eyes. "It was fun to watch," she said. "But my little slave can't have all the excitement."

"Mistress?" I asked.

She stood with her legs spread apart, and motioned for me to come over. "Pleasure me, slave," she ordered. "From the ground up."

I rushed over to lie happily between her feet. I didn't often have the pleasure and I always loved to hear the order. I started slowly, the way she wanted me to, licking her shiny black leather boots. The musty taste was sugary sweet to me.

"Polish them good," my Mistress warned. I felt the

tip of her riding crop trace a design on my bare ass and I knew I would feel its sting if I didn't meet her standards. I licked all over her foot and when she raised it, I took the stiletto heel into my mouth, sucking on it. I then worked my way slowly up the boot until I finally reached her creamy thigh. I continued licking carefully on my way up to her delicious pussy.

When I was far enough up, I realized that the tight suit had a zipper which opened the crotch. I held my breath as I pulled it open, marveling at the first sight of her dark hairs and fleshy lips.

I parted them with my tongue. Kneeling before her, pushing my tongue straight into her, I touched her clit with each stroke. I knew better than to tease her with soft caresses, and I licked hard at her hot button. The crop resting lightly on my back and the heavy collar around my neck reminded me that I had to do everything just as my Mistress preferred.

Her pussy was hot and wet and I licked greedily. Her salty-sweet taste was like honey to me. "That's a good, slave," she whispered, and I was filled with pride knowing that she was enjoying it.

It didn't take long for her to come. I lashed my tongue over her clit and was rewarded with the soft moan and the tight muscles that signified her orgasm. Her cunt quivered and I kept my tongue on it until the last spasm was over. Then I sat back.

She zipped the suit closed again and walked away. I watched her every move with rapture. My Mistress just excited me so much; I would have done anything for her if she had commanded it.

She sat in a wingback chair near the dining room. "Clean that mess up," she ordered. Quickly I picked up the empty champagne glasses and took them to the kitchen. From her seat she watched me as I washed and dried them carefully and put them away.

"Now come here," she said. I did. "Lie down on the floor, on your stomach." Again I obeyed, and she got up and walked into her bedroom.

When she came back out some time later, she looked more like a businesswoman than a domineering mistress. The tight suit and leather boots were gone, replaced by a well-cut suit. The only clue to her role in the apartment was the pair of heavy chrome handcuffs she carried.

She bent down and snapped one of the cuffs on my wrist. The other was closed around the leg of the chair.

"I have to go out now," she said. "I expect that I will find you in this position when I get back. Am I right?"

"Yes, Mistress," I said. There simply was no other answer.

I watched her as she walked to the door. I heard the key turn in the lock and realized that she could be gone ten minutes, or twelve hours. I had no way of knowing.

One thing was sure, though. My arm was going to cramp up and I was going to be sore after lying on the floor. My shoulders would hurt even more where she had beaten me with the riding crop. But my eyes would not leave the door, and my position would not change all the time she was gone. My Mistress had commanded it, and no matter how long it took, that was how I would wait for her return.

THE SECRET ROOM

"A glass of red wine, please."

"Right away," the waiter said, and hurried to get it. Jennifer smiled. She didn't know if it was her voice, or her bearing, her attitude, or a combination of all three, but people always seemed very eager to carry out her wishes.

Most of them did it because she asked them to. A few did it because she told them to, in no uncertain terms, and with terrible consequences if they did not. She was sitting waiting for one of these.

It was a favorite trick of hers. She would call up one of her submissives and tell her to be at a restaurant at a specific time. Jennifer would then arrive fifteen or twenty minutes early, so that when her slave arrived, she would already have a few sips of her wine gone and the submissive would know that her mistress had been sitting for a while waiting for her. All submissives knew that keeping a mistress waiting was not a very good idea, of course.

Jennifer didn't do it every time, for she liked to keep her submissives on their toes with different tricks. One woman had actually caught on to the waiting game, and had arrived at the restaurant half an hour earlier, so that she was the one sitting waiting when her mistress came in. Jennifer was secretly amused that she had figured it out, but she took her home and beat her for it anyway, to teach her that slaves should never try to outsmart the mistress.

The waiter set the glass in front of her. She picked it up and took a sip; it was very good. She looked at it thoughtfully. Burgundy always seemed like such a cruel color to her. It was the color of flesh struck repeatedly by a hand or a whip, or the shade of marks left on the skin by handcuffs.

She shivered in anticipation of her plans for the day. She was waiting for Elizabeth, a submissive who had been coming to her for several weeks. She was still very inexperienced, but eager to learn; a tiny brunette woman who was fitting into her role very rapidly. When she had first come to Jennifer, through a mutual friend, she admitted that she had never been with a dominatrix before but that she had been completely turned on by reading stories about domination. There was no doubt that the real thing completely lived up to her fantasies, for Jennifer knew that no one could fake the shattering orgasm that Elizabeth had experienced the first day, her wrist bound together and her ass burning from a spanking with a wooden hairbrush that she had earned.

She sipped her wine, and checked her watch that she kept in her pocket. It was shortly after noon. When she used this trick, she always hid her watch and made sure she wasn't seated near any clocks. That way, the submissive would never know. She also gave them very exact times, such as eighteen minutes past the hour or thirteen minutes to, and handed out punishments for being early that were just as cruel as those for being late.

Elizabeth came in at exactly the time Jennifer had given her. She watched as the tiny woman spoke to the waiter, then followed him to the table. She was surprised to see Jennifer already seated, her glass half empty, and she stood silently behind the chair. She didn't yet know the significance of the half-empty wineglass between her mistress' fingers. "Bring her a Scotch, neat," Jennifer told the waiter, who nodded and left.

She looked up at Elizabeth. "You are late," she said.

Elizabeth's face went deathly white and her eyes grew large. "No, Mistress!" she protested, quietly, so that other diners would not hear her. "I checked my watch, Mistress!"

"Sit down," Jennifer commanded, and Elizabeth slipped quickly into the chair. She looked coldly at the young woman. "Are you implying that I don't know what time it is?"

Elizabeth looked down at the table like a scolded child. "No," she said.

"No?" Jennifer's eyebrows went up.

"Oh—no, Mistress!" Elizabeth quickly added. "I'm sorry, Mistress, I honestly thought I was on time."

"I'm sure you did," Jennifer said. "But obviously you didn't check carefully enough. No matter, you will pay for it later."

"Yes, Mistress," Elizabeth said. Her cheeks were blazing. Jennifer knew it was a combination of shame and excitement.

The Scotch arrived. Elizabeth looked at it warily. "I don't like Scotch, Mistress," she said.

Jennifer leaned over the table and spoke in a low, icy voice. "I don't give a good goddamn what you like or don't like," she said. "I ordered it for you, and you will drink it. You are already to be punished for being late. Do you want to add to your suffering by being disobedient?"

"Oh, no, Mistress," Elizabeth said. She sipped the amber liquid, making a face as she did so.

Jennifer went into her bag for a cigarette, which she lit with her gold lighter. Elizabeth's eyes never left her. She smoked it until there was a long ash on the end of it.

She looked around. "There doesn't seem to be an ashtray on this table," she observed.

"I will get you one, Mistress," Elizabeth said quickly as she started to get up. She sat back down at a swift motion from her mistress.

"That won't be necessary, Elizabeth," Jennifer said. "Hold out your hand."

Elizabeth looked frightened as she did. Jennifer casually flicked the ash into her outstretched hand. By the time the cigarette was almost finished, there was a small gray pile of it in her palm.

"Now eat it," Jennifer ordered.

Elizabeth looked at her, horrified, but did not dare say a word. After a long pause, she lifted her hand slowly to her mouth and licked the ash off. She swallowed heavily and took a hefty drink of the Scotch. For a moment she looked like she was going to be sick, but finally composed herself. She stared in terror at the end of the cigarette between Jennifer's fingers. When Jennifer reached over to the empty table beside them for an ashtray and stubbed it out, she let out a huge sigh of relief. She had no doubt that Jennifer would have extinguished it in her hand just as calmly.

Jennifer motioned for the waiter and paid for the drinks. She waited until Elizabeth had finished every swallow of the hated Scotch, then walked out of the restaurant. Elizabeth meekly followed several steps behind.

They went out to the parking lot, where Jennifer's dark blue Lincoln was waiting. She opened the doors, and Elizabeth obediently got into the back seat. Within minutes they were on the highway, heading for Jennifer's house. Elizabeth lived only a short distance from her mistress, and the trip to the restaurant had taken several buses and the better part of the morning. Jennifer knew this, and basked in the knowledge that her submissive had traveled all that way just to have a drink she didn't want and a ride back to almost the same spot she had started out from.

Her pussy felt hot as she glanced in the rearview mirror at the woman sitting in the back seat. She had a whole stable of them, women who would obey her every command no matter how bizarre. The power she held over them was incredible. She enjoyed laying traps for them just so that she could punish them when they were taken in by them. No matter how cruel her discipline, they waited anxiously for her to summon them again, and showed up punctually wherever she told them to be.

There were other benefits as well. Her house was always spotless and her chores always done for her, with only a spoken order. She also remembered the old days, before she had given herself over to her role as a dominatrix. Sex had always required the age-old game of introductions, drinks and dinners, conversation and uncertain kisses, and after all that, chances were good that she'd end up frustrated anyway. Not anymore. Now if she wanted sexual satisfaction, she simply commanded a submissive to give it to her.

They arrived at the house and Jennifer drove into the garage, the automatic door closing behind her. She opened the door leading into the house, but this time, she searched her key ring for another, smaller key. This was going to be a very special afternoon for Elizabeth.

On previous occasions, Elizabeth had stayed on the main floor of the house while she learned her lessons from her mistress. The trip to the restaurant and been a final test, for Jennifer knew that if she had put up with the inconvenience of traveling that far, she would do anything. She was now ready to see the true side of her mistress. The hairbrushes and the padded shackles were upstairs. The real toys were kept elsewhere.

Instead of going into the living room, Jennifer led the way into the cellar. Elizabeth looked a bit puzzled but followed her silently. There, Jennifer used the small key to open the lock on a door. She swung it open and led her submissive inside.

Elizabeth gasped. She had never seen anything like it before. It was Jennifer's secret torture room, her masterpiece, a collection that had taken several months to assemble. It was magnificent.

The floor was cold concrete, painted black, as were the walls. One wall was almost completely covered by a huge mirror. Another wall was hung with dozens of devices—whips, handcuffs, chains, dildos, straps, gags, and bondage clothes and masks fashioned out of leather and rubber. There were heavy rings screwed into the walls at all heights, and a few were in the ceiling and floor. There was a wooden frame with various lengths of chain on it standing against one wall, and a padded sawhorse. A leather sling hung from the ceiling. There was also a comfortable-looking padded chair in one corner, and Elizabeth instinctively knew that it was the one piece of equipment in the room that had never been used by a slave. It looked almost like a throne and stood on a small platform. Jennifer let her stand in the middle of the room for a long time, looking around and taking everything in. Once again, her cheeks were flushed and her expression was a mixture of complete terror and raw, overwhelming sexual desire.

"Take your clothes off," Jennifer ordered. Still looking around her, Elizabeth quickly shed her clothing. From the wall, Jennifer took a pair of heavy chrome handcuffs. She made Elizabeth sit on the cold floor next to one of the heavy rings, and quickly shackled her to it. Then she turned off the light, throwing the windowless room into complete darkness, and left, closing the heavy door behind her.

Once upstairs, Jennifer took her time. She wanted Elizabeth to fully experience complete captivity, without knowing what would happen or even when her mistress would come back to get her. She undressed and ran a bath, fragrant with perfumed oil, and relaxed in it for half an hour. She toweled herself off, then stretched out on her bed and looked through a magazine. All the time, she imagined the woman in her secret torture room. She would still be hunched on the icy concrete floor, unless she had risen to her feet, but that would have meant standing while bent double; the handcuffs wouldn't let her lift her hand more than a few inches from the floor. She would see nothing but the velvet darkness, for there was no source of light to allow her to see shapes even vaguely. She would be able to hear the running water and the footsteps on the floor above her, but would have no idea what her mistress was doing. Perhaps she even needed to use the toilet and would have to suffer with a full, painful bladder.

She was becoming more and more excited by the suffering she had inflicted on the woman in the cellar. Her pussy was throbbing now, and she put her hand between her legs and touched her clit. Slowly her touch became a soft caress, and then suddenly she was rubbing hard, the white-hot rushes filling her belly.

Her fingers were creamy with her juice, and they glided swiftly over her hot flesh. She was squeezing her naked tits and playing with her nipples with her other hand as she thought about what she was going to do when she went back downstairs. In her mind's eye she was spanking that sweet little ass with a leather paddle, and for every blow, she tweaked her torrid clit.

She came, her whole body shivering with the tingling spasm that coursed through her. She leaned back on the pillow, but instead of feeling relaxed, she was so excited she could hardly wait to get downstairs. Her orgasm had just whetted her sexual appetite. She wanted to slip fully into her role as the cruel dominatrix with her slave chained below her.

She selected a costume from her closet and got dressed. It was one of her favorites, a laced leather cat suit that exposed her breasts and was cut so high in the legs it barely covered her pussy. She slipped on high patent leather boots with stiletto heels that were so shiny they reflected the light. She touched up her makeup, accentuating her large green eyes and painting her lips her favorite cruel burgundy color. Then she smoothed her hair and walked to the stairs.

When she snapped the switch in the dark room, Elizabeth closed her eyes quickly against the bright lights. She was still on the floor where Jennifer had left her. Jennifer noticed with satisfaction that her skin was covered with goosebumps and that her fingernails had a milky blue tinge.

She retrieved the tiny key and unlocked the handcuffs, then ordered Elizabeth to stand up. Her ass was deathly white where it had been pressed against the concrete floor. Jennifer decided that it could use some warming up.

"Come here, slave," she said, and led Elizabeth over to the padded sawhorse. She selected two leather cuffs from the wall display and buckled them around her captive's wrists. She then picked out a length of heavy chain, with snap closures at either end.

Elizabeth obediently held out her hands, as she had been taught to do, and Jennifer secured the cuffs on her wrists. They were heavy and studded, with metal rings on them. They looked huge on Elizabeth's tiny arms.

Roughly she pushed Elizabeth from behind so that the woman was bent over the length of the sawhorse, her feet on the floor. She snapped one end of the chain to one wrist, wrapped it around the sawhorse leg, and attached it to the other wrist. Elizabeth could not get up or stand straight.

Elizabeth watched her, eyes wide, as she walked over to the wall to make a selection. She stood for a long time deliberating, as if she were in front of her closet trying to decide which dress to wear for a party, or what song to play on the jukebox. Finally she selected a wide leather paddle, its face covered with rounded metal studs.

She walked back and ran her hand gently over Elizabeth's exposed ass. The skin was still uncomfortably cold. "Elizabeth," she said, "do you remember what happened in the restaurant?"

"Yes, Mistress," Elizabeth whispered.

"I don't like to be kept waiting," she said. She caressed her ass again, this time with the side of the paddle. The leather glided over her skin as soft as a kiss. "A slave shouldn't keep her mistress waiting, should she?"

"No, Mistress," Elizabeth whispered.

Once again the paddle whisked over her flesh, only this time she felt the icy metal studs. Jennifer smiled as she watched Elizabeth's ass cheek muscles tighten with the touch. She could see her pussy, and the lips were glistening with hot juice. She had given Elizabeth a "safe word," but she doubted if she would ever hear her use it. Her punishment was turning her on as much as it was exciting Jennifer.

"Look to your right, Elizabeth," Jennifer ordered, and the small woman did. They were looking into the huge mirror. "I want you to keep watching it. I want you to see what happens to slaves who disobey their Mistresses. You will see it, and you will feel it."

She watched the mirror herself and loved what she saw. A well-built woman, wearing tight leather clothes and high shiny boots, standing before her shackled slave. She lifted the studded paddle. She admired herself for a moment longer, then brought the paddle down hard on Elizabeth's ass.

Elizabeth screamed, then sobbed. Her ass went flaming red, and the imprints of the studs were clearly visible on her skin. She went limp and screwed her eyes up tightly as the pain seared through her.

Jennifer stood back. "That won't do at all," she said. "Most slaves don't yell as much as you do. I don't want to listen to that crap." She went back to the wall and returned with a rubber ball gag which she roughly stuffed in Elizabeth's mouth and buckled at the back of her head. Elizabeth almost choked on the musty rubber taste. Her eyes were brimming with tears.

Jennifer brought the paddle down again. Elizabeth's cries were effectively muffled by the rubber ball that forced her mouth open and then filled it. Jennifer smashed the paddle across her ass four more times. Elizabeth's tears were now streaming down her face. Her ass cheeks were horribly red and raw, and her legs trembled uncontrollably. But her pussy was even wetter than it had been before.

Jennifer went back to the wall and carefully hung the leather paddle on its hook. She had an assortment of them, but this was one of the nastiest of all with its biting chrome studs, and was her favorite. She stroked its wide flat surface for a moment with her hand. The studs were still warm from Elizabeth's ass.

She turned to Elizabeth, who had watched her the whole time. "Now that I think about it, slave," she said coldly, "I also recall that there was a small problem with the drink I ordered for you."

Elizabeth's face was white and her eyes looked like a rabbit's caught in a pair of car headlights. It was obvious that she had either forgotten the episode with the Scotch, or hadn't realized its significance. In any case, she certainly hadn't expected to be punished for it.

Jennifer walked over to her and softly stroked her cheek with a long, lacquered fingernail—her favorite cruel burgundy. She knew her gentle touch would be like icy fire to her captive. "Everything a mistress does for you is in your best interest," she said. "I know what is good for you and you must trust me. If I order you something to eat, then you must eat it. If I order you something to drink, then you must drink it. If you don't, then I must take that as a sign of disobedience."

She took a few steps beside the sawhorse and gently stroked the vulnerable naked back. "It seems that you didn't think your mistress knew what was best for you when she ordered your Scotch," she said. "Basically, your attitude said 'fuck you.' Well, that is exactly what I will do."

She selected a particularly large dildo from the wall, attached to a leather harness. Elizabeth watched her as she strapped the harness around herself. She looked in the mirror with satisfaction. The large rubber dick stood out straight from her mound. She picked up a tube of jelly and greased its large head thickly.

Elizabeth watched her until she positioned herself behind her captive; the tiny woman then turned to look at her in the mirror. Jennifer rubbed her ass cheeks gently, then spread them. She put the head of the dildo against the tight rosebud of Elizabeth's ass, and then pressed her hips in.

Elizabeth's cries were once again muffled by the rubber ball gag. Jennifer pushed the dildo until it was halfway in. Then she slowly fucked Elizabeth's asshole with it.

The view in the mirror was delicious. Her slave was shackled to the sawhorse, a strap around her head to hold her gag in place, and the huge dildo was up her ass.

"You like my dick in you, don't you, slave?" Jennifer whispered. Elizabeth didn't nod her head quickly enough, and Jennifer grabbed her hair and yanked it, pulling her head back. "That wasn't very enthusiastic, slave," she hissed. She let go, and Elizabeth, fresh tears on her face, nodded rapidly.

"That's better," she crooned. She was pumping faster now and the greased dildo was sliding in and out of Elizabeth's tender asshole. "I'm glad that you like my dick. I like to see it fucking you."

Despite her obvious pain, Elizabeth was evidently enjoying it very much too. She kept her eyes on the mirror, where she could see Jennifer slamming the dildo into her. She whimpered through the ball gag with every thrust, but she also couldn't deny the fact that her pussy was throbbing and incredibly hot and wet.

Deeper and deeper the dildo slid, until it was almost entirely in Elizabeth's tight ass. Jennifer loved the rocking motion of her hips as she pumped the heavy rubber dick in and out. Occasionally she slapped Elizabeth's ass cheeks hard with the palm of her hand. The skin was still mottled red from her paddling with the studded leather.

Finally the dildo was in as deep as it could go. Jennifer pumped it in and out a few times, then pulled it out entirely. Elizabeth went limp as the huge dick slipped out of her sore asshole. Jennifer kicked her ankles until she spread her feet wide apart. Then Jennifer rubbed the rubber cockhead on her exposed clit.

Elizabeth immediately lifted herself on her toes so that the dildo could press fully against her swollen love button. This time she moaned, muffled by the gag still tied in her mouth. Jennifer rubbed it hard against her.

She was so excited she came almost immediately. Jennifer walked away while she was still trembling and moaning, and unstrapped the dildo. Without even looking back at the woman who was still chained to the sawhorse, her mouth distended by the nasty gag, she switched off the light, closed the door and went back upstairs.

She called the restaurant where she had met Elizabeth earlier in the day, and made a reservation for herself for a late dinner. Stripping off the leather suit and the high boots, she enjoyed a long, hot shower, then styled her hair and dressed carefully in a tight skirt and a shirt that showed off her beautiful breasts and large nipples. She returned to the secret room more than an hour after she had left Elizabeth down there.

Again her captive screwed her eyes tightly closed as the bright lights were flicked back on. Jennifer unbuckled the ball gag, and Elizabeth worked her jaw stiffly, her tongue licking her parched lips. Once the leather cuffs were taken off, she straightened up slowly and with difficulty.

"I have an appointment, slave," Jennifer said, hanging the cuffs and the chain back up in their spot on the wall. "Pick up your clothes and come with me."

"Yes, Mistress," Elizabeth said, and gratefully followed the dominatrix up the stairs. The carpeted floor felt soothing under her feet, which were white and numb from standing on the cold concrete floor of the secret room.

Jennifer led her captive to the bathroom, where she started a shower for her using only cold water. "Get in," she said.

Elizabeth started to climb into the tub, until she felt the icy water sting her skin. "Mistress, it's cold!" she protested.

Jennifer slapped her as hard as she could on her cheek. "I'm not stupid, slave!" she cried. "I know it's cold. Do you think I can't tell the hot water tap from the cold one? Now get in there, before I chain you to the faucet and leave you in there."

Elizabeth whimpered as she closed the glass shower doors behind her. She tried to stand in the far end of the tub, as far away as possible from the cold water, but on Jennifer's orders stood under the shower head and soaped herself.

"I'm finished, Mistress," she said once the soap was rinsed away.

Jennifer was sitting in the small chair that fitted under the bathroom vanity. "I don't really care, slave," she said. "I'll decide when you're clean enough. Now soap yourself again. You're filthy." She watched as Elizabeth lathered herself a second time and stood under the freezing cascade of water to rinse herself off.

She left Elizabeth for a few more minutes under the shower, then gave her permission to turn off the tap and get out. Elizabeth slid the shower door open and looked longingly at the huge, fluffy bath towels that hung from the rack on the wall. Instead, Jennifer gave her a small, thin hand towel and she struggled to dry herself with it. She was shivering violently and her fingernails and lips were blue.

"Hurry up," Jennifer warned, as Elizabeth scrubbed at her hair with the small, damp towel. She was actually running about an hour early, but it gave her great satisfaction to see Elizabeth fumbling in her haste.

She gave Elizabeth an old comb from under the sink to fix her hair, then led her into the living room where she made her crouch on her hands and knees on the sofa.

"Is your asshole still sore, Elizabeth?" she asked.

"Yes, Mistress," the tiny woman replied.

"Very good," Jennifer smiled. "I was hoping that he dick wouldn't be too small for you." She disappeared into the bedroom and came out with an object in her hand. Elizabeth craned her head to see, but Jennifer slapped her ass hard and told her to keep her eyes straight ahead.

It was a small butt plug, made of rubber with a flared, round base. Jennifer squeezed some lubricant out of a tube onto it, and then pushed it slowly into Elizabeth's tightly puckered hole. Elizabeth's moan, a mixture of pain and pleasure, sent sweet erotic shivers through her.

"Now, slave," she said, "I am going back to the restaurant where you met me to have my dinner. I am taking you back there, and you can find your own way home. All the time you are traveling home, you will wear this butt plug. You will wear it until I send for you again. You will wear it to work, and when you are sitting at home. You will wear it when you go shopping and when you are eating your meals. You may take it out when you wash or use the toilet, but you must put it back in right away afterward. The next time I see you, this plug will be in place. Do you understand?"

"Yes, Mistress," Elizabeth groaned. Her ass was already distended and sore from the dildo, and the butt plug aggravated it, but she loved the delicious full feeling and the knowledge that her mistress would have complete control over her even when she was alone.

"If I see you and that plug isn't in you, then I have a much larger one," Jennifer continued. "I won't use lubricant on that one. You will wear the larger one until I am finished with you, and then I will take it out and stuff it in your mouth. Do you understand that I am very serious in this command?"

"Oh, yes, Mistress!" Elizabeth cried. "Yes, Mistress. I will not disobey."

"Good," Jennifer said. "Now get dressed. If I'm

late for my dinner, I might think about using the larger plug on you right now."

Elizabeth pulled on her clothes, wrinkled from lying on the floor, and Jennifer led her out to the car. She sat low in the back seat to relieve the pressure on her painful ass.

Jennifer slipped behind the wheel and headed for the highway nearby. Once on it, she pushed the gas pedal sharply, and the big engine responded immediately. Jennifer smiled. She loved taking control, even over machines. It thrilled her to know that she alone harnessed the huge car that was capable of such high speeds. It thrilled her, too, to know that she controlled the woman in the back seat, who looked out of the window with an expression of discomfort. The butt plug must hurt like hell, and she was excited by the knowledge that Elizabeth would put up with it until she heard from her mistress again—whether it was a few hours or several days—simply because she had been ordered to do so. Jennifer had no doubt that her orders would be carried out to the letter. She didn't know how long she would make her wait, and decided she would think about it later.

She got off at her exit and pulled into the parking lot of the restaurant. As she turned off the engine, she watched a bus pulling away from the stop across the street.

"That's your bus, isn't it, Elizabeth?" she asked.

"Yes, Mistress," the woman replied miserably.

"How long until the next one?"

"Forty-five minutes, Mistress," Elizabeth replied.

Jennifer turned in the seat to face her, with a kind expression, and for a moment Elizabeth thought she might be invited into the restaurant to share dinner with her mistress. Her hopes fell immediately. "At least you're lucky there's a bench there," Jennifer said. "You won't have to stand up for the whole time you're waiting."

They got out of the car, Elizabeth moving slowly and stiffly. Suddenly an old expression popped into Jennifer's head, one that her mother used to say all the time: "She walks like she's got a bun up her ass." She had to smile. How true it was!

"I will get in touch with you later," Jennifer said. "In the meantime, you won't forget my orders, will you?"

"No, Mistress," Elizabeth said. "May I have permission to speak?"

"Yes, slave," Jennifer granted.

"I love you, Mistress," Elizabeth said.

Jennifer touched her cheek. "That's good, slave," she said. Then she turned and walked into the restaurant. Elizabeth stood by the big Lincoln for a long time, then made her way through the parking lot to the bus stop. It would be two or three hours before she finally got home.

Jennifer stood in the foyer. The waiter who had served her earlier noticed her right away, and led her to a table by the window. She sat down and ordered a drink, and noted with satisfaction how quickly the young man rushed to fill her order.

She looked out the window, and saw Elizabeth sitting on the bench by the bus stop. She thought about it for a moment, and then decided to make her wait at least a week.

WEEKEND AWAY

The sun was just coming up as Louise started the car and waited for Meg to come out of the house. The air was warm already and the sky was clear; it was going to be a beautiful day. They would be at the cottage before noon, and the rest of the weekend would be theirs.

The cottage belonged to Meg's brother, and although the two women had stayed there several times as his guests, it was the first time they would be there alone. Stephen's office was going through a major restructuring and he would be putting in a lot of hours, so he wouldn't be able to get away to the cottage for quite a while. He phoned and told them to go up and enjoy themselves for the long weekend. Louise intended to. She loved the cottage, a simple structure set well back from the road on the shore of a small, lonely lake. Stephen owned a large chunk of the surrounding woods and in all the times they had visited, they had never seen another person. It was as far away from civilization as she could possibly imagine. It also had no luxuries—unless a wood stove and a manual pump in the kitchen could be considered a luxury—but Louise and Meg both enjoyed their rugged weekends away.

Finally Meg came out, the last bag of groceries in her hand. She stowed it in the back seat, then got into the front seat and leaned back. "Ready for takeoff, commander," she said, and arranged her long, honey-colored hair into a ponytail.

Louise backed out of the driveway and they were off. There was no traffic on the road this early and they were out of the city shortly, heading up the eight-lane highway that would soon merge into four, and finally into two, past fields and sleepy farms and independent little towns and hamlets.

Louise happily reached over to tweak Meg's nipple. She was wearing no bra, and the touch felt so good. Both of them enjoyed fishing and walking through the woods, but most of their anticipation was for a weekend at a cottage where no one would see them. They had plans to make love on the porch, in the grass, under the trees, maybe even out in the boat.

Around ten they stopped in their usual spot, the last town before the turnoff for the cottage. It wasn't really even a town, just a gas station and a general store, but the store sold cones filled with generous scoops of rich ice cream and it was considered a grave sin to drive by without stopping for one. They sat out on the front steps of the store eating them, and Louise's eyes stayed on Meg the whole time she ate hers. Meg licked hers slowly, with long, cool laps of her small pink tongue, and Louise couldn't help imagining her pussy in place of the strawberry ice cream and Meg's tongue licking slowly and carefully around her hungry, swollen clit.

Ten miles past the store they turned off the main road onto a dirt one, and five miles later onto a path that was just two wheel ruts cut into the forest floor. It was only used by people going to the cottage—most people drove by it without even noticing it was there—and small branches that had grown since Stephen's last pruning brushed against the sides of the car. They had to drive slowly since the path was bumpy and uneven. The trees grew together overhead and the sunlight through them dappled the hood of the car.

They finally reached the clearing where they parked the car, and that was when they regretted every extra item that they had packed away. Everything had to be carried the last half-mile to the cottage along a narrow footpath. Their complete privacy didn't come without a bit of hardship along the way.

Their loads were heavy, but they were able to take everything in one trip, the cooler shared between them. After the city, the woods were pastoral and almost silent except for bird songs and the rustle of the leaves when the breeze shook the trees. The path seemed three times as long as usual, and they were sweating by the time the woods finally opened up and the lake and the cottage were in sight.

They dropped their gear on the front porch and opened the door. The cottage was closed and stuffy and they opened the windows to let the cool breeze through. It was only two rooms, a bedroom and a combination kitchen, living room, and dining room with a convertible chesterfield bed. The bathroom was the little shack close to the trees.

They went into the bedroom, where the double bed was neatly made, with an extra blanket draped over the foot. Louise couldn't wait any longer. She reached for Meg and hugged her, then parted her lips for a kiss.

Meg was just as eager as she was, and thrust her tongue inside her lover's mouth. She touched Louise's pussy through her shorts and could feel the heat of her flesh through the fabric. Louise moaned and reached down to press Meg's hand hard against her horny cunt.

Louise reached for the tail of Meg's T-shirt and pulled it over her head, exposing her lovely tits. She eased Meg onto the bed and licked each nipple slowly, relishing the warm, salty taste of her skin. Her hot, sweaty skin, so out of place in the sanitized city, was real and natural out here in the quiet cottage with its surrounding woods. They kissed as Meg reached under Louise's shirt to feel for her warm tits.

Louise stood up and quickly pulled her clothes off. It felt so good to be out of them, since they were damp and clinging. The cool breeze coming through the open window felt delicious on her skin, and her nipples went hard. Meg begged her to bring them closer, and she sucked them into her mouth one at a time, circling them with her tongue and biting gently on them.

Louise unzipped Meg's shorts. Meg lifted her ass off the bed and Louise pulled off her shorts, along with her panties. Her blonde cunt was moist and inviting. Louise stroked her inner thighs softly, then ran her fingers over the sweet flesh between Meg's legs. Meg sighed and opened her legs wider. They were both relaxed now that the city and the long drive were behind them. In this secluded world of no telephones, newspapers or televisions, they could take as long as they wanted to do anything. It wouldn't bother either of them at all if a single orgasm took all day to achieve.

Louise crawled onto the bed and Meg moved up on the pillows to make more room for her. She stretched out with her head between Meg's thighs, and lazily licked the length of Meg's creamy pussy. Meg sighed and closed her eyes.

Louise lapped at her slowly. She poked her tongue into the tight hole, spreading it gently with her fingers so that she could reach in as far as possible. Her lips were wet with Meg's sweet juices. She moved up to Meg's clit and ringed it with her tongue several times, then pushed it back and forth with just the tip. She gave several quick butterfly flicks over it and returned to Meg's hole. Meg groaned as the soft wet tongue parted her pussy lips and pushed deep inside her.

Again the probing tongue moved up to her clit, and this time, Louise stayed there. She licked slowly but with a lot of pressure, grinding her tongue against Meg's sweet button. Meg moaned louder, and Louise licked faster and sucked the clit into her mouth. As she held it firmly between her lips she lapped her tongue quickly against the edge of it. Moaning and trembling, Meg slipped into a smooth, luscious orgasm. Louise licked her hard and fast and she cried out as hard spasms rocked her and a tingling wave coursed through her body right to the ends of her fingers.

"Mmmmm, that was so good," Meg purred. She took Louise's hand and pulled on it. "Come up here, you, it's your turn."

Meg looked so comfortable lying on the bed, her head deep in the fluffy pillow, that Louise knew there was no way she was going to get her to move. Instead, she got up on her knees and crouched over her blonde lover's face, her dark pussy right above Meg's mouth.

Meg may have looked sleepy, but that was all. Immediately she pushed her tongue into Louise's cunt and licked all over it. She held Louise's ass and pushed her back and forth over her outstretched tongue, pressing deep into Louise's hole and the glistening folds of her lips. Her tongue fitted perfectly into the cleft of Louise's pussy. She licked slowly and steadily, and Louise thrilled to the hot little torrents that coursed through her body and made her so warm.

"Oooh, that's nice!" Louise gasped, and moved her hips so that Meg's tongue touched every tender little crevice of her pussy. She loved it when Meg licked up both sides of her clit teasingly, and then moved in to rock it back and forth until she couldn't take any more. She could feel the tongue gliding up the sides and then hit the center. Her whole pussy felt tighter and tighter, the pressure building up in her belly and even in her legs. Then she gasped and cried out as Meg's tongue sent her hurtling over the edge. Her whole body followed into her stunning climax and she collapsed on the bed beside Meg, panting for breath.

Meg held her closely until she calmed down. They lay together on top of the blanket, as the cool breeze dried the sweat on their bodies and the pussy juice on their lips. Louise was so comfortable she could hardly believe it. Just yesterday she had been running around the office like a madwoman, trying to get things done, answering the phone that never stopped ringing, making decisions, giving orders. Now she was lying in her lover's arms, completely fulfilled from her orgasm. The only sounds were the droning of heat bugs and the melodic tones from the wind chimes that hung on the front porch.

She had almost dozed off when Meg shook her awake. "Come on," she said. "All that stuff's still out on the porch, and I don't want to have to find the refrigerator in the dark."

They got up and reached for their clothes, then looked at each other and smiled. They didn't even have to wear clothes up here if they didn't want to. Giggling like children, they went out on the porch naked to bring the gear inside.

Meg took the cooler and went off to put its contents away. The "refrigerator" was an invention of Stephen's, devised one day when he found an icy cold spring bubbling up out of the ground some distance uphill. He came back the following week with a heavy coil of rubber hose, which he inserted at the spring and snaked down to a shady area under the trees. There he attached the end firmly to an old enamel cream can. Foods requiring refrigeration were packed in bottles or sealed plastic containers and submerged in the cold water that constantly flowed into the cream can. Meg filled the can with milk, plastic containers of cold cuts and cheese, and a few cans of beer. She filled a water jug from the hose and headed back to the cottage, stopping for a moment to pick a large handful of the colorful wildflowers that Louise loved so much.

She got back and helped Louise with the rest of the unpacking, after setting the wildflowers in an old milk bottle on the kitchen table. Both of them were still excited at having the cottage to themselves. The novelty of doing their unpacking naked was an event in itself, and they stopped for a moment to enjoy a hug and a long kiss that promised many more encounters like the one they had just had.

Once everything was put away, they decided it was time to clean up. They walked down to the lake hand in hand with a bar of soap and bottle of shampoo. The water was cool, and at first they made a game of it, splashing each other as they stood in the shallow water. Then Louise got the bar of soap and rubbed it over Meg's body. Her soapy hand moved smoothly over Meg's skin. She took a long time soaping Meg's breasts. She cupped each one and rubbed the bar of soap over the nipple, back and forth, while Meg moaned softly and watched the ends of her tits grow hard and big.

She took forever to wash Meg's pussy. She slid the bar of soap over the curly blonde hairs and then rubbed the soap in with her fingers. She would have been happy to spend hours with her hand in Meg's cunt. She loved to run her fingertips over the lips, to tickle the clit and push gently at the entrance to her hole.

Meg took the bar of soap away and turned Louise around to soap her back. She ran her hands between the softly rounded cheeks of Louise's ass, sending warm thrills through her. She soaped Louise's pussy from behind, touching her clit and pulling her hand all the way back to tease gently at her tight ass. She reached around to soap Louise's breasts, and the two of them stood in the knee-high water for a long time, Meg's tits pressed tight against Louise's back, her hands playing with Louise's nipples, all the time kissing and sucking at the sun-warmed neck that she loved so much.

Eventually Meg felt the soap drying on her skin, and she took Louise's hand and led her farther out into the water until they could dive below the surface and swim around. The lake was crystal clear and the bottom was smooth and sandy, perfect for spending a lazy, hot afternoon. They swam out a considerable distance and then raced each other back. Louise won by a narrow margin. Laughing and panting, they got out and stretched out on the grass to let the sun dry them off. It was too much trouble to walk back to the cottage for a towel. Meg fell asleep, but Louise spent the time looking around, admiring the tall trees and the birds that flitted among them, the cloudless blue sky, and the lake that stretched almost motionless to the opposite shore. She also took a long time to admire Meg, who lay in the grass beside her, her beautiful tits boldly naked, her stomach flat and her blonde triangle warm and inviting.

Louise began to feel hungry, and she woke Meg up. The two of them walked back to the cottage. They were so rested and relaxed that neither of them felt like doing anything and were grateful for the pre-pared supper sitting on the ice left in the cooler. Louise remembered how she had insisted on bringing the coolers, over Meg's protests that they would enjoy cooking their first meal at the cottage by them-selves. Louise rubbed it in until Meg picked up a cushion off the sofa and threatened to start a pillow fight.

It was too nice to sit inside, and they ate on the table that sat on the huge porch running the whole length of the cottage. They opened containers of salad and unwrapped their sandwiches, and after-ward had slices of pie and glasses of buttermilk. In the city they preferred to cook exotic dishes and go to expensive restaurants as often as their budget per-mitted. Out here, their simple meal enjoyed in the warmth of the early evening tasted better than the dishes at their favorite French bistro.

After cleaning up, they got out their books and sat in the rocking chairs on the porch, and read until it got too dark to see. A light would have brought the mosquitoes, and neither of them wanted to go inside. Fortunately, one of Stephen's first additions to the cottage was an old-fashioned swing that hung on chains from the roof of the porch. They sat together like young lovers, instead of companions of almost fifteen years, and watched the full moon and the evening star rise up over the lake and cast magical reflections in the dark water. Louise snuggled into Meg's shoulder and thought that if the world ended that night she would have no regrets.

Soon the rest of the stars came out and they marveled at how the same sky that looked so bleak and gray against the city's lights could turn into a stunning light show that dwarfed everything below it here, only a few hours away from the city limits. The air was filled with the chirping of thousands of crickets.

They eventually went into the cottage, and Louise lit the lamp and put it on the table. They pulled a pack of playing cards out of a suitcase and opened two cans of beer. They played cards accompanied by the soft hiss of the lantern and the sound of moths banging against the screen windows, attracted by the light.

Meg looked up and watched Louise carefully as she waited for Louise to play her card. The soft light of the lantern lit Louise's face beautifully, making her look as soft and romantic as a painting. Meg couldn't believe how lovely she looked. Both of them were always so busy with a variety of real and imagined responsibilities that they seldom had time just to sit together for a full day and enjoy each other's company. Even their vacations were usually sightseeing expeditions with as much crammed into each day as humanly possible. But at this cottage there were just the two of them, without a care in the world and nothing that had to be done if they didn't feel like doing it.

At the moment, Meg decided that even the game they were in the middle of could wait. She put her cards on the table, took Louise's away from her, and laid them down also. Then she picked up the lantern, took Louise by the hand, and led her into the bedroom.

The moon was so bright it cast shadows in the room, and Meg extinguished the lantern. They had both put on light cotton robes before dinner, and Meg untied Louise's and let it fall open. Louise's breasts looked like rich cream in the moonlight. Meg licked them as if they were. The nipples reminded her of wrapped candy kisses and she sucked on them slowly, letting them slide through her lips as she pulled her head back. Louise sighed with the pleasure.

"That feels so nice," Louise said. "Come up here and kiss me." Meg straightened up and put her arms around her lover. They kissed slowly and deeply, with a sudden passionate longing that surprised them both. Meg felt like she was tasting Louise's mouth for the very first time. Louise responded to her touch and pushed her tongue deep into Meg's mouth, probing with an awakened urgency that their earlier, lazy lovemaking had only begun to tap.

Meg's hand was cupped over Louise's dark triangle. She could feel the heat on her fingers. She glided over Louise's clit, and her fingers came away wet and slippery. Thrilled, she returned Louise's kiss eagerly and probed the depths of the hot, hidden treasure between her legs. When she could wait no longer, she knelt down on the floor in front of Louise and kissed her belly, then moved down to where the dark hair began. She teased the cleft of Louise's pussy by blowing softly on it, and then she used her tongue to push the lips apart and skim over her clit.

She tasted warm and woodsy from their swim in the lake. Meg was no longer relaxed; she was aroused and feverish. She wanted to feel Louise tremble and hear her cry out. She wanted to sink as deeply as she could into the pussy she was licking.

Louise moaned and spread her feet apart. Meg crouched under her and pushed her tongue into Louise's hole. Louise moved up and down on it, fucking Meg's tongue as if it were a warm dildo. Meg's cheeks were wet with her pussy syrup. She wished she could climb right up inside her.

Louise rocked her hips so that her clit slid back and forth over Meg's outstretched tongue. Meg flicked it back and forth. She focused on the swollen little knob, and Louise groaned. Her spine was quickly turning to jelly as Meg lapped at her.

"You're going to make me come," Louise warned, and Meg doubled her efforts. Louise did as she had promised. Her orgasm was intense, and she gasped, then cried loudly as it overcame her. She sat down on the edge of the bed, and Meg followed her. She carefully licked her lover's dark pussy until every drop of her honey-sweet juice was gone.

Meg's pussy was throbbing so badly she could hardly stand it. "Lie down," she whispered huskily. She straddled Louise's thigh and rubbed her pussy hard against it. She hadn't done this for a long time, and had almost forgotten how raw and delicious it felt.

Her tits swung back and forth as she ground her pussy on Louise. Louise reached up with her hand

and brushed Meg's erect nipple with each stroke. It was a gentle touch but it was fiery hot to Meg. She moaned and moved harder and faster.

"Feels so good," she panted. Louise reached with both hands, holding Meg's breasts firmly and kneading them with her fingers. Meg felt almost dizzy. Her hot pussy was building up to a tremendous orgasm as she rode Louise on the bed. Her long hair hung around her shoulders, swinging with each move. Every touch of Louise's hand on Meg's nipples sent thrills through her and made her cunt even more sensitive.

She almost screamed when she came. She leaned forward onto Louise and the two of them hugged tightly, kissing passionately. At that moment, the cottage could have burned down around them but they would not have let go of each other.

"I love you so much," Meg gasped, and Louise kissed her and whispered her love too. Meg rolled over onto the bed, but they stayed in each other's arms and fell into a deep, dreamless, sleep holding each other tight.

Louise woke in the morning to the sounds of movement in the other room. The bedroom was still fairly dark. She looked at her watch and groaned; five o'clock. Getting up in the middle of the night had to be a trait of Meg's family, she decided; when they had shared the cottage on other weekends with Meg's brother, he and Meg had been up before dawn to go fishing or hiking. Louise had been much happier staying in bed until a considerably more civilized hour—ten, perhaps.

She clutched the pillow until her eyes finally stayed open by themselves, then she got up, pulled on her robe, and wandered into the other room. The bedroom was somewhat chilly, but the kitchen was warm. Meg had a fire going strong in the wood stove, and on top Louise could see a coffeepot, a skillet of eggs, and slices of bread toasting on the hot surface.

Meg was smart enough to hand Louise a cup of black coffee before she even spoke to her. "I've got breakfast under control," she said. "You go out and wait on the porch."

She did, and was instantly happy that she had gotten out of bed. The sun was just coming up over the lake, which was as smooth as a mirror. The morning mist was rising off of it in slowly moving wisps. The sun reflected brilliant red on the water, and then its light was caught by the millions of tiny dewdrops on the grass. Louise breathed deeply and caught the smell of wet earth and pine trees. She took a sip of her coffee and decided that all was right with the world.

Meg came out shortly afterward with their breakfast. She loved cooking and saw the wood stove as a special challenge. Generally her results were good, although perfect bread baked in the little compartment on the side of the stove still eluded her. She had been trying for years and had finally managed to get one side of the loaf raised and baked to a golden brown. Usually they settled for biscuits baked in a covered skillet.

Even out in the middle of nowhere, Meg's cooking retained its little touches. The eggs were fried with onions and peppers, and there was a small jar of brandy butter for the toast. The sun cleared the tall trees on the far side of the lake as they ate. The sky was cloudless; it was going to be a beautiful day.

"I want to go fishing," Meg said as they took their dishes inside and Louise pumped water to wash them.

"Sounds good to me," Louise said, and added a bit of hot water from the kettle on the stove to the dishpan. Within minutes the kitchen was clean, and they went into the bedroom to change.

The lake was so smooth they hated to disturb it. Stephen didn't want the sound of any motors disturbing the forest, so there was only a rowboat. They stowed their tackle box, rods, a small cooler, and a thermos of coffee, then pushed away from the shore. They had flipped a coin earlier, and Louise got the task of rowing out to the middle of the lake.

Once they were some distance from shore, Meg dropped the anchor overboard, and they got ready. For Meg, it meant selecting the proper lure for casting and retrieving. Louise's preparation consisted of putting a worm on her hook and dropping it over the side, the rod held between her knees, while she poured a cup of hot coffee from the thermos and adjusted the cushion she sat on. Casting was fine, but she couldn't see the point in wasting a perfectly good day with work when there was a container of coffee and a box of worms in the boat.

They enjoyed themselves so thoroughly that time just slipped by without notice. Louise even got to smirk a little when her lazy way of fishing put three bass on her stringer compared with the single one Meg had caught. Meg didn't mind; she was busy running through recipes in her head, deciding what would be the best way to prepare them for dinner.

The sun crept higher in the sky, and they began to get very warm. Her little thermos empty, Louise went into the cooler and got a cold soda for each of them.

The overhead sun beat down on them, and Meg's light shirt was sticking to her. "It's too hot just to sit out here," she said, reeling in her lure and setting her rod down in the bottom of the boat. "I'm going for a swim. Are you in or out?"

"In, of course," Louise said, and watched with interest as Meg unbuttoned her shirt. She looked around, but as usual, there wasn't another soul on their little part of the lake, which was surrounded almost entirely on three sides by heavy woods and the single cleared area where the cottage stood. She took her shirt off and draped it over the boat seat. She looked at Meg, who had her shirt off too. Her skin was hazy with a thin film of sweat and Louise thought her nipples looked delicious.

In a single, sinewy motion, Meg wriggled out of her shorts. As always, Louise loved the inviting look of her rich blonde pussy. Meg saw her staring, and she smiled and ran her fingers between her legs. "I like what you're thinking," she purred. "When we get back to the cottage, I want an instant replay of last night."

She got up and moved carefully so as not to upset the boat, and slipped into the water. She came over and held onto the side of the boat, pushing her wet hair out of her eyes. "It's a lot colder out in the middle than it is on shore!" she said. "It sure feels nice. Are you coming in or are you going to sit there all day?"

Louise pulled off her thin cotton pants, then sat on the edge of the boat and fell backward into the water. It was shockingly cold at first, then refreshing.

It was still a novelty to be in the lake without bathing suits, and they swam back and forth and treaded water, then dived below the surface. The sunlight filtered through the clear water in long shafts toward the bottom.

Louise held her breath and swam under the surface. She could see the large, dark shadow of the boat, and the movement of Meg's arms and legs as she treaded water. As she got closer, she could see Meg clearly, her pussy too sweet to be passed up. She surfaced right in front of her, running her hands over her body on the way up, and kissed her hard.

Meg returned her kiss. They were close to the boat, and they grabbed the heavy nylon rope attached to the anchor to hold themselves up. Close to each other, they kissed again and wrapped their free arms around each other's necks.

The sensation was unlike anything they had felt before. The cold water contrasted with their warm bodies, and there was no resistance at all when they touched each other. There was nothing but water below their feet, and it was easy to move up or down just by loosening their grip on the rope.

Meg slipped below the water, and Louise felt her nipple being sucked into her mouth. After the cold water, Louise's mouth felt fiery-hot and almost dry. She sighed as she felt Louise's tongue slide over her rock-hard nipple and flick it back and forth. When she finally let go and came up for a breath of air, the rush of cold water on her breast sent shivers through her.

She reached for Meg's tits. The cold water had made the nipples as hard as her own, and they felt like little marbles to her hands. She tweaked them and rolled them between her fingers, then held each breast in her hand and massaged them slowly and lovingly. All the while, they kissed, their tongues slipping into each other's mouths and mingling with one another.

The feelings were so delicious, they had to share them. Meg reached out her free hand and touched Louise's breasts under the water. She could see them just below the surface, and they looked even bigger and harder through the water. She was fascinated.

She watched her hand as if it belonged to someone else, holding Louise's tits and rubbing them, and enjoying the feeling of Louise's hands on her own nipples at the same time.

Gradually their hands strayed farther down. "Your pussy is so wet," Louise said, and Meg groaned loudly at her pun and put her hand between her lover's legs.

It felt so different from anything they had enjoyed before. Louise's pussy lips were chilled from the water. Meg ran her finger between them, onto her clit, which was a bit warmer. Then she slid her finger effortlessly into Louise's tight hole, which was deliciously warm and velvety smooth. Louise moaned and ran her fingers over Meg's clit.

They both held onto the anchor rope as they felt each other. Their pussies were cool from the water, but the rushes that went through their bodies were like liquid fire. Meg could feel Louise's clit growing larger and getting firm, and she knew that her own was doing the same thing. She could feel every movement of Louise's fingers as sharply and as clearly as if she were watching them. She moaned as Louise stroked her from her clit right back to her hole and finally up to her sweetly puckered ass.

They were both moaning as their hands explored every inch of each other's cunts under the surface of the water. The water lubricated their hands, and they slipped effortlessly over their fleshy cunts. Their bodies floated weightless in the water, adding to the sensation. It felt almost unreal to them. Imagine, swimming naked in the middle of a lake, out in the wilderness, with their hands in each other's cunts, feeling each other up—marvelous!

Louise came first. She moaned and gasped as her orgasm warmed her water-chilled body. She kept her hand in Meg's cunt, and the blonde woman came a few moments later. She was so excited by coming in the cold water that she let go of the anchor rope and slipped below the surface. She quickly came back up, gasping and panting both from the water and her explosive climax.

They hugged again and exchanged tiny kisses. Then they both took advantage of their new-found energy to swim back and forth around the boat and dive as far down as they possibly could. With some difficulty, Meg finally got back in the boat and helped Louise to climb in as well.

Both of them sat naked on the seats until they dried off enough to put their clothes back on. Indeed, if it hadn't been for the fear of sunburn they would have preferred not to put them on at all. It still felt new and exciting to sit up straight in the boat with nothing on. In the city, there was always the feeling that someone could be watching, and pulling curtains and closing blinds was a way of life. Out here, surrounded only by trees and birds, they could do whatever they wanted, in any stage of dress or undress they liked.

"I'd like some lunch," Louise said, and Meg agreed. She fitted the oars into the oarlocks while Louise pulled up the anchor and the stringer of fish. Then she rowed back to shore.

Louise sat back lazily, one hand trailing in the water, as they neared the cottage. It was almost noon, and everything seemed laid back and sleepy, even the birds. After lunch they might put up the double hammock and just nap in each other's arms, or hike up the shady path between the trees.

She looked over at Meg, rowing the boat back in, and smiled with love for her. Their weekend away, alone together, had been the best idea they could have possibly imagined, and it still wasn't even half over.

Across the calm water she could hear the heat bugs droning in the sunlight. She thought about the money they had saved, with no particular goal in sight. She decided that over lunch she would ask Meg her thoughts on looking for a lonely cottage all their own.

Orgasms are healthy.

(and they feel really good, too.)

THE LIMOUSINE

$7.95

n.t. morley

ISBN 0-9716384-4-6

Luscious Brenda was enthralled with her roommate Kristi's illicit sex life: a never-ending parade of men who satisfied Kristi's desire to be dominated. While barely admitting she shared these desires, Brenda issued herself the ultimate challenge — a trip into total submission, beginning in the long, white limousine where Kristi first met the Master. Following in the footsteps of her lascivious roommate, Brenda embarks on the erotic journey of her life.

THE PARLOUR

$7.95

n.t. morley

ISBN 0-9716384-3-8

The Parlour is a hot new take on a classic fantasy-or two! For those with dreams of service to a sexy, powerful couple, look no further.

—Carol Queen

A beautifully dark and wonderfully erotic tale, The Parlour succeeds admirably what so many erotic novels can only try to be: a story of sex and power to the nth degree.

—M. Christian

JUDITH BOSTON

$7.9

titian beresford

ISBN 0-9716384-6-

A new, unexpurgated edition! Naughty Edward's compulsive carnal experime
never go unpunished by the severe Judith Boston. Edward would be lucky
get the stodgy companion he thinks his parents have hired for him. Instead,
exquisite woman arrives at his door, and from the top of her tightly bound b
to the tips of her impossibly high heels, Judith Boston is in complete contro

CINDERELLA

$7.9

titian beresford

ISBN 0-9716384-1-

"A wildly decadent and completely original erotic fairy tale"
—Dr. Pascale Solange

A Magical exploration of the erotic potential of this famous fairy tale. Titi
Beresford triumphs with castle dungeons and tightly corseted ladies-in-waitir
naughty Viscounts and impossibly cruel masturbatrixes-nearly every conceival
method of kinky arousal is explored and described in vivid detail. A fetishis
dream and a masochist's delight.

MASTERING
MARY SUE

$7.95

mary love

ISBN 0-9716384-0-3

Mary Sue is a rich nymphomaniac whose husband is determined to pervert her, declare her mentally incompetent, and gain control of her fortune. He brings her to a castle in Europe, where, to Mary Sue's delight, they have stumbled on an unimaginably depraved sex cult!

THE VIRGIN

$7.95

alison tyler

ISBN 0-9716384-5-4

Does he satisfy you? Is something missing? Maybe you don't need a man all — maybe you need me. I know I need you.

Veronica answers a personal ad in the "Women Seeking Women" category — and discovers a whole sensual world she never knew existed! And she never dreamed she'd be prized as a virgin all over again, by someone who would deflower her with a passion no man could ever show…

MAN WITH A MAID $7.9

anonymous   ISBN 0-937609-25-

"Great erotic fiction begins and ends with this novel."

—Evergreen Reviev

The ultimate epic of sexual domination. In the "snuggery", a padd
soundproofed room equipped with wall pulleys, a strap down table, and a ch
with hand and leg shackles. The untiring pervert, Jack, bends beautiful Alice
his will. She corrupts her maid and her best friend into lesbianism, then
three girls lure a voluptuous mother and her demure daughter into the snugg
for a forcible seduction and orgy. Perhaps, the all-time hottest book!

THE BLUE ROSE $7.9

alison tyler   ISBN 0-9716384-8-

Alison Tyler's words evoke a world of heady sensuality, where fantasies
fearlessly explored and dreams gloriously realized.

-Penthouse

The tale of a modern sorority - fashioned after a Victorian girl's school. Igni
to the heights of passion by erotic tales of the Victorian Age, a group of lu
young women are encouraged to act out their forbidden fantasies - all under
tutelage of Mistresses Emily and Justine, two avid practitioners of hard-c
discipline!

ALEXANDER **TROCCHI** $7.95

thongs

ISBN 0-937609-26-9

Spain, perhaps more than any other country in the world, is the land of passion and of death. And in Spain life is cheap, from that glittering tragedy in the bullring to the quick thrust of the stiletto in a narrow street in a Barcelona slum. No, this death would not have called for further comment had it not been for one striking act. The naked woman had met her end in a way he had never seen before — a way that had enormous sexual significance. My God she had been...

TABITHA'S TEASE $7.95

robin wilde

ISBN 0-9716384-9-7

"If you have ever fantasized about being dominated by a sorority of beautiful college women, then used as their sex toy, then this is the book for you."
—Mistress Solange

When you're a helpless male captive of the notorious sorority girls of Tau Zeta Rho, you're in for a deliciously devilish week of the most exotic and erotic torments these imaginatively wicked co-eds can devise. And if you get the infamous Tabitha as your tormentrix, you'll find yourself hovering on the excruciating edge with each new perverse twist of her insatiable imagination. Think it's a man's world? Guess again. With Tabitha around, no man gets what he wants until she's completely satisfied—and maybe, not even then.

ORDERING IS EASY

orders can be placed by calling our toll-free number
PHONE: 800.729.6423/FAX: 310.532.7001/E.MAIL: magic-carpet-books.com
or mail this coupon to:
Magic Carpet Books
15608 South New Century Drive
Gardena, CA 90248

QTY.	TITLE	NO.	PRICE

e never sell, give or trade any of our customer's names

SUBTOTAL	
POSTAGE + HANDLING	
TOTAL	

the U.S., please add $1.50 for the first book and 75¢ for each additional book;
Canada, add $2.00 for the first book and $1.25 for each additional book.
reign countries: add $4.00 for the first book and $2.00 for each additional book.
rry, no C.O.D. orders.
ase make all checks payable to Magic Carpet Books
yable in U.S. Currency only. CA state residents add 8.25% sales tax.
ase allow 4-6 weeks for delivery.

Name: _____

Address: _____

City: _____ State _____ Zip _____

Telephone: [   ]_____

E.mail: _____

Payment: ☐ check ☐ money order ☐ visa ☐ mc ☐ amex ☐ discover ☐ diners club

Card No: _____